P9-BYO-251

My Brother, THE ROBOT

My Brother,

Dutton Children's Books
NEW YORK

THE ROBOT

BY BONNY BECKER

Library of Congress Cataloging-in-Publication Data
Becker, Bonny.
My brother, the robot / by Bonny Becker.—1st ed.
p. cm.
Summary: When his father buys a SIMON Robot, advertised as "the perfect
son," Chip decides that he can't compete with his new brother, but in the end,
the whole family learns that perfection may not be so great after all.
ISBN 0-525-46792-0
[1. Robots—Fiction. 2. Fathers and sons—Fiction. 3. Science fiction.] I. Title.
PZ7.B3814 My 2001
[Fic]—dc21 2001028693

Published in the United States 2001 by Dutton Children's Books,
a division of Penguin Putnam Books for Young Readers
345 Hudson Street, New York, New York 10014
www.penguinputnam.com

Designed by Alan Carr
Printed in USA
First Edition
1 3 5 7 9 10 8 6 4 2

To Karen, Kurt, Ann, Lisa, and Odette, with love

My Brother,
THE ROBOT

"We don't want to pressure you, son. But we've ordered the Perfect Son. He's arriving today."

"What?" I squawked.

"Yes," said Dad. "We've ordered the SIMON Robot—the Perfect Son. Actually, he's a factory second. But twenty percent off!"

I couldn't believe it. They'd fallen for those dumb ads on TV.

Get a SIMON! The Perfect Son!
He cleans his room. He says "sir."
He laughs at Dad's jokes. He gives Mom hugs!
Yes, it's Simon the Robot. You'll never have to apologize to the neighbors again. Order yours now.

"You're replacing me with a robot?!"

"We're not replacing you, Chip. Think of Simon as your swell new brother."

Dad tried to make it sound good, but he wouldn't look at me. He thumped the remote control to change the channel on the media center and pretended to laugh at something he saw on the screen, but his laugh sounded fakey, like pebbles rattling around in a can.

Finally he cleared his throat and said, "The truth is, your mother and I hope he'll be a good example for you."

I hunched my shoulders. Now I knew what this was all about. Couldn't they just forget about me almost flunking the fifth grade? I mean, the key word here is "almost."

"You flunked the fifth grade?!" Dad had croaked when I handed him my report card a week ago.

Mom turned pale.

"I didn't *flunk,*" I said. "I just have to go to summer school."

Along with all the other loser dummies, I'd added in my head. My voice had gotten kind of shaky. You'd almost think I was going to cry or something lame like that, but it's not my fault everything's so hard.

They didn't have to make such a big deal out of it. I mean, a robot to show me how to do things right? Maybe some kids would think it was cool, but I hadn't even met Simon yet, and all I wanted to do was punch him in the nose.

Just then the doorbell rang, and Dad sprang up from his chair.

"That must be Simon now."

Sure enough, there on our tiny front porch was a huge box plastered with the picture of a happy family and the words: GET A SIMON! GET HAPPY.

"I think this is a mistake," I said.

"Nonsense," said Dad, and he made me help him drag the box in.

"If he's so perfect, why doesn't he drag himself in?" I grumbled.

"He can't be activated until he's struck by sunlight," said Dad, cutting through the tape around the box.

"Where's he going to sleep, anyway?" I asked.

"Your room."

"My room!"

"OK, stand back."

"Wait!" Mom ran in from the back room, pulling off her reading glasses. "Don't start yet."

Dad cut the last piece of tape, and the sides of the box fell open like the petals of a lotus flower opening to the dawn. Simon the Robot sat in the center on a metal folding chair.

He didn't look like a robot. He looked like a regular boy with neatly combed brown hair, a bow tie, and a calm, superior sort of look. He looked like flesh and blood. Only his eyes were closed, and his skin was the color of a dead worm that's been washed out by rain.

"Dad, did you ever see the movie *The Killer Robots*?"

"Chip, Simon is here to help you and that's that."

"It'll be a good learning experience," said Mom, but her smile was a little uncertain. I bet getting Simon was mostly Dad's idea.

"OK," Dad said. "Let there be light."

He pulled back the curtains on the living room window. As though it were planned, the clouds outside parted, and a ray of pure white sunlight fell into the room and right on Simon.

His skin began to ripple. It was creepy—like a sheet rippling in a breeze. I guess some weird robot fluid was pumping under the skin. Then his chest rose and fell. His first breath.

His eyelids popped open. His eyes were blue and as blank as a piece of plywood. There was nothing he saw and nothing he thought. His hands, clenched into fists on his thighs, opened.

He blinked and stood up.

Simon the Robot was alive.

He walked over to my mom and gave her a nice hug.

"Why, thank you, Simon," she said, looking surprised.

Simon walked over to my dad and shook his hand. "I want to be just like you, sir," he said.

"Welcome, Simon," said Dad.

Simon looked at me.

"Who's he?"

"That's your brother, Chip," said Dad.

Simon frowned. "The company didn't tell me I would have a brother."

"Well, that's what you're here for, Simon," said Dad. "We want you to set an example of excellence for Chip."

"Oh." Simon looked me up and down.

"Well, I'll try," he said.

"What's that mean?" I cried.

Only no one was listening to me. Mom and Dad were giving Simon a tour of the house.

"And here's the family room," murmured Mom, who hated housework but was proud of the orange wallpaper she'd managed to put up herself and the brown fake-leather couch that stuck to your legs on hot days. The plastic leather only had a couple of rips, and Mom had patched those very neatly with brown tape.

"Complete with a Corvex 2020 Media Center," said Dad, sweeping his hand in the direction of the wall-sized screen. It was secondhand, of course, and featured only five hundred channels. You couldn't program it to stop on keywords or anything.

Everything in our house was like that. Dad loved getting the latest, coolest things, but to save money, he always got these so-called bargains, but then you had to thump them to make them work, or the leg would fall off or something.

Simon gave a short laugh. A mean kind of laugh, really. A laugh that seemed to say, "Wow, what a crummy place."

"I beg your pardon?" Mom said.

"Hmmmmm." Dad frowned.

But then Simon did the perfect thing. They didn't call him the Perfect Son for nothing. He pointed at IT—the giant silver trophy that stood in the middle of the bookshelf.

"What's that, sir?" asked Simon.

"That?" said Dad, like it was no big deal. "Oh, that's just my trophy for when I beat the Speedos off Butch Neeman to win the All-City Ten-to-Eleven-Year-Old-Boys Swim Championship of Eastville."

Beside IT was room for a second giant silver trophy. *My* giant silver trophy, for when I supposedly won the All-City Ten-to-Eleven-Year-Old-Boys Swim Championship of Eastville this summer.

My dad was a great swimmer when he was a kid, and he keeps hoping I'll be good, too. But the truth is, although I can swim OK, I'm not that fast. Not fast enough to win medals or anything.

But every weekday in the summer, Dad takes me to morning workouts, even though it means he's late for his job at the Post Office. Then he goes to the meets in the evenings. Even when I only get a third place in the butterfly, he smiles, pats me on the back, and says, "Good job."

He's always been pretty proud of anything I do, even when it's nothing special. Only this summer . . . well, I think he's beginning to figure out that me winning the All-City Ten-to-Eleven-Year-Old-Boys Swim Championship of Eastville is never going to happen. Not in *this* universe.

And he doesn't seem so proud anymore.

"Wow!" said Simon, admiring the trophy. "That's swell."

It was weird how he used the same words Dad used. Words like *swell*. I wondered if they were specially programmed for their owners or something.

Dad cleared his throat modestly. "Thank you, Simon. Now then, let's show you your room."

He led the way down the hall and flung open the door to my room.

"Oh!" Simon drew back with a gasp.

"Is everything all right?" asked Mom.

"It's messy," said Simon, like he'd found a hideous new form of life that he never knew existed. "There's stuff all over the floor. The bunk beds aren't made. There are rotting half-eaten apples in the corner and dirty clothes everywhere."

"It's no big deal," I said. "Look." I quickly picked up a few clothes, shoved some junk deeper under the bed.

Mom and Dad didn't look too pleased. My room was kind of a sore point.

Simon did that mean laugh thing again.

"I simply can't allow this to pass for cleaning up your room. Really, I must ask you to step aside."

Which I did, mainly because Dad made me.

Simon went to work.

He moved at blazing speed. Garbage flew into a large plastic bag he seemingly produced from thin air; clothes were sorted, folded, and put away with laser-like precision.

"Sheets," he called out to Mom, who ran to the linen closet.

"Vacuum cleaner," he cried, snapping out his hand. Dad passed the Hoover over to him like a runner passing the baton.

In no time at all, my room was perfect. Everything was put away; the bunk beds were made. It was dusted, polished, vacuumed. And I didn't have to do a thing.

Maybe a Simon Robot wasn't so bad after all.

But then Simon announced he would take the top bunk.

"That's *my* bunk," I said.

"Now, Chip," said Dad, "cooperation."

And then Simon took over half the closet and half the dresser drawers and half of my desk, which was really just a flat door on top of some shelves.

"Good work," declared Dad.

"Doesn't it look nice," said Mom, following him out the door. "Time for dinner, everyone."

Simon glanced my way as he left the room.

"You're not so special," I said low, so Mom and Dad couldn't hear.

"No," he said. "Just perfect."

Then he smiled, and a bit of perfect sunlight glinted off his perfect teeth.

I noticed a piece of lint on the carpet.

"Hey, look!" I cried. "He missed some dirt."

But no one was there to hear.

"Well now, Simon," said Dad. "Tell us a bit about yourself."

It was dinnertime, and we all sat at the table, wolfing down Mom's meatloaf. That is, Dad and I wolfed it down. Simon cut up everything carefully; he swallowed before talking, and he didn't shove the mashed potatoes onto his fork with his fingers, like some people I could name.

Simon must have noticed, too, because he kept looking over at Dad, until Dad clenched up his left hand beside his plate, trying to stop himself from pushing food with his fingers. That's when he asked Simon to tell us about himself.

Simon set down his fork, dabbed his mouth with his napkin, and cleared his throat.

"Well, sir, as you know, I'm made by Cyborg Corporation. *DING! Ding, ding, DONG! Extraordinary*

Products for Ordinary People. DONG!" He chimed out the Cyborg slogan just like the TV ads.

"I represent the first line of truly humanoid robotic products," he continued in his regular voice. "My full name is the Simonson XX, the Xcellent Xample Model." He glanced pointedly at me. "To all outward appearances, I'm human, but of course, I'm better."

Simon said this as if it was the most natural thing in the world, but all the humans at the table looked a bit uncomfortable.

"That's nice, dear," Mom said, trying to smooth things over. "Do you have any family?"

And then she must have realized that sounded dumb.

"Oh dear, I guess you wouldn't, would you?"

"I have a Creator. Dr. Kurt Simon. I was manufactured at our Des Moines plant on Assembly Line 340. A Miss Odette Overmyer was quality-control inspector that day, so I suppose you could call them my mother and father, but really, you are my family now."

Mom reached over and patted Simon's hand.

"Surprisingly lifelike, isn't it?" Simon commented pleasantly about his skin. "I am made with the latest in advanced synthetic life technology. My coating is a highly specialized skinlike polymer (patent pending). I am, of course, completely waterproof and fully guaranteed for all parts and labor for thirty days."

Waterproof!

"Hey, wait a minute," I said. "Can robots swim?"

Dad's eyes slid away from mine, and he did that fakey laugh again. "Well, ha, ha. What an interesting question. Er, *can* you swim?"

"Of course, I've never actually tried swimming, being only one hour, seventeen minutes, thirty-nine seconds, and eight milliseconds operational. But the Simonson XX is designed to learn and excel at all activities."

"Tell you what," said Dad, "tomorrow morning is swim-team practice. Chip and I can take you to the pool, and you can try swimming. See what you think."

"Excellent, sir," said Simon, jumping up to help Dad clear the table.

"That was the best meatloaf I've ever eaten," he told Mom.

Which was easy enough for him to say, since it was the *only* thing he'd ever eaten.

"Chip, plenty of daylight left," said Dad. "How about getting in some work on Mrs. Cranston's yard?"

Oh, yeah. Mrs. Cranston. That was one more little thing that had gone wrong this spring. I was riding my bike, and I noticed this great little hill in Mrs. Cranston's yard. I shot down the hill, jumped the edge of her driveway, and flew really high. It was like riding a monster motorcycle.

It was really fun, only Mrs. Cranston's new grass was coming in, and I tore her yard all up. Now I had to help her with her garden all summer.

"Mrs. Cranston is our next-door neighbor," Dad explained to Simon. "Chip is helping her with her yard."

"Helping a neighbor," said Simon. He seemed to scan something flickering inside his head, then spoke as if reading a dictionary. "Considered a sign of maturity and kindness. A good thing to do."

"Chip is making up for a previous error," Dad said.

"Error?" Simon did that scanning thing again, paused, and looked shocked. "Oh. I see," he whispered, like it was too awful to even say out loud. "A mistake."

"Don't you even know a word like *error*?" I snorted.

"We don't really need to know," said Simon, "since we don't make any. But even so, our programming is deliberately 'fuzzy.'"

Dad nodded like he knew what that meant.

"It means," said Simon, "that our learning is somewhat random. This gives our new family the joy of 'teaching' us, as if we are not actually perfect, which we are, but still there is the illusion that we are like human sons, who, of course, need a lot of instruction."

Again he looked at me.

"We're very proud of Chip," Mom said. "We just hope you can give him some, well, motivation, I guess. Everyone can benefit from learning."

"Of course," said Simon without sounding like he meant it.

Then he picked up a couple of plates and headed for the kitchen.

Dad followed.

"You'll be interested in our sonic dishwasher," I heard Dad saying. "Got a great deal on it. Cleans the dishes with sound waves, only it's not working quite right. The dishes keep exploding . . ."

I slouched outside and over to Mrs. Cranston's house.

Mrs. Cranston is about a thousand years old. She has white, wispy hair and big hands with thick blue veins. She doesn't have any kids, and her husband died a long time ago. She lives in a little house with a neat green lawn and a big, leafy garden full of flowers that is about the most important thing in her life.

I wondered how she felt about living next to us after my dad poured concrete on our yard and painted it green.

"Low maintenance," he always explained proudly when visitors asked.

"Over here, Chip," Mrs. Cranston called when she saw me.

She handed me a long kind of garden fork and told me I could dig up dandelions from the grass—again. That's all I ever did. She didn't trust me to weed the flower beds.

Digging dandelions isn't too bad if the ground is wet. I like to wiggle the fork down deep near the root and see if I can pull the whole thing out like a long, thin white carrot. But when the ground is dry, like tonight, it's not so much fun.

I wriggled and inched and tried to pull up each weed gently, but no matter what, the root would snap off in the middle. It didn't take me long to give up and just start snapping.

"Please get the whole root," she said.

"Yes, Mrs. Cranston." I inched up the next dandelion as slowly and carefully as I could. I noticed a worm wriggling away from the hole I was digging. I picked him up and gently set him in the soft dirt of the flower bed. The worm probably thought a miracle had happened to him.

"I was lost in the desert," the worm cried to the horde of worms gathered around him. "I was a stranger in a strange land. I—"

"Chip." Mrs. Cranston pointed her trowel at me. "The dandelions."

"Yes, Mrs. Cranston." I have this bad habit of daydreaming.

I set back to work.

"I noticed a Simon box on your front porch," she said.

"I have a brother now." I scowled.

"A robot for a brother?"

"Yeah, he looks like a human, except he wears a bow tie and he's perfect."

"How dreadful."

"Yeah, I didn't even know they still made bow ties."

"No, I mean how dreadful to be perfect," she said, vigorously shaking the dirt from a clump of grass she'd pulled from the flower bed.

I stared at Mrs. Cranston. She had lived before there were robots or computers. She had lived even before there was TV! She'd seen a lot, I supposed. Old people are supposed to be wise, but she never looked wise to me, just crabby, and she smelled old—a dry, powdery sort of smell—and so even though I sometimes thought I might ask her things, whenever I smelled her old smell, I just felt kind of discouraged and never did.

So I didn't ask her about it being dreadful to be perfect, but it seemed to me that it couldn't be right. It would be great to be perfect.

If I were perfect, I would win all the swim races, and everyone would clap and cheer, and my mom and dad would think I was wonderful. I'd do all my homework on time. I'd know all the answers. I'd be the best at everything at school. I'd win all the talent shows. I'd be picked first all the time. In fact, I'd be the one doing the picking. I'd be better than everyone! What could be better than that?

"Chip!" Mrs. Cranston pointed her trowel at me, again. "Dandelions."

"Yes, Mrs. Cranston."

I dug back in.

B*RIIIINNGGG!!! BRIIIINNGGG!!!*

I jolted upright and bonked my head on the bunk above me. Where was I?

Simon thrust his head over the side of the top bunk, and I remembered. I had a brother now. I had the bottom bunk now.

"Rise and shine," he said. He opened his mouth and let out a really annoying ring like an alarm clock.

I covered my ears.

"I have a number of attractive alarm options," he announced.

He started to go through them. Various ding-dongs, and pings, and several local radio stations.

"What time is it?" I groaned.

"Western Daylight Saving time is 7:02 A.M. And twenty-four seconds."

Seven o'clock! I slumped back on my bed. This

was practically inhuman, but then I remembered, Simon wasn't human.

"Wake me in a couple of hours," I mumbled, and tried to go back to sleep.

Simon, however, hopped out of bed and began to touch his toes. Then he did about one hundred push-ups and several lunge sort of exercises. Then he got dressed in the clothes he had arrived in, which he had put neatly away the night before. He brushed his light brown hair until every strand shone, straightened his bow tie, and then sat in my desk chair and stared at me.

"Aren't you getting up?"

I sighed but crawled out from my sheets, pulled on my jeans and T-shirt, which had been lying in a heap on the floor, and yawned.

"That's it?" asked Simon. "That's all you're going to do?"

"Well, I have to go to the bathroom."

"Oh, that's right." He did that mean laugh thing again. "I'd forgotten how inefficient humans are at energy processing. A lot of waste product, I've been told."

I went to the bathroom. I tried to be fast, but I seemed to have been a very inefficient energy processor the night before and had a lot of waste product to take care of.

When I got back to my room, Simon was busy rearranging my collection of plastic action figures.

"They're not in alphabetical order," he sniffed. "Oh, and I threw out your comic books."

"Hey! You can't do that."

"Your father wants me to set a good example. From now on, you and I can study the inaugural speeches of various U.S. presidents and compare the speeches to their actual records."

"What?" I groaned.

"Now," he went on crisply, "tell me about this swimming thing."

I glanced over at him. "You really don't know?"

Simon shook his head.

"OK, well, you get in the water and you stretch out on the water, flat, on your stomach—"

"Yes." He nodded sharply, his eyes snapping back and forth as he took in the data.

"And that's it," I said.

"That's it?"

I nodded. I tried not to smile and rub my hands and cackle with villainous glee, because, with any luck, if Simon got in the water and just lay there—well, he'd sink like a big, fat stone.

"Isn't this grand!" Dad strode out of the locker room and onto the pool deck at the Westerwood Community Pool.

Westerwood Community Pool was a big outdoor pool surrounded by a wide, scratchy cement deck and then brownish grass. In the afternoons, the grass is checkered with moms on striped beach towels and the pool is full of screaming kids, but in the mornings, the swim team works out and the team has the pool to itself.

Dad nodded to Coach Benjamin, who was busy yelling at some of the other swimmers, and took a deep breath. "Aaah, the smell of chlorine," he said. "Reminds me of my youth."

"Yes, sir," said Simon.

"My days as swimming champion," he continued. "The day I won All-City. When kids were kids and men were men."

"How grand, sir," said Simon.

"OK," said Dad. "Let's see what you can do. Chip, you go in there with him. Let's have us a little race."

I jumped into the water at the shallow end. Simon followed. He wrinkled his nose a bit when some drops of water splashed on his perfect hair.

"So I just stretch out flat on this?" he asked.

He patted the surface of the water like a baby.

I nodded, and then, so I wouldn't feel totally guilty after I totally crushed him, I looked up at Dad and said, "Are you sure? I mean he's never swum before."

"On your marks," said Dad.

I shrugged and grabbed onto the pool edge with one hand. Simon watched me and did the same.

"Get set."

I stretched out my other hand and got ready to push off with my feet. Simon did, too.

"Go!"

I pushed off hard.

Glancing back, I was surprised that Simon was nowhere in sight. Then I looked down. There he was, on the bottom of the shallow end, just lying there like a submerged log.

Oh, too bad. I dug in and headed for the other end and victory.

And then suddenly, there he was. Beneath me. Underwater, at exactly the depth he had sunk to in the first place. He now crisply moved his arms and legs, and with each movement, he shot forward. He was like a torpedo!

I desperately thrashed my arms and legs, swimming as hard as I could, but it was no use. Simon beat me to the other end by a half-dozen strokes.

Dad had raced around to that end of the pool.

"He's a natural!" he cried.

"He's three feet underwater," I pointed out. "And besides, he's a machine. He's not 'natural' at anything."

Dad reached his arm into the water as far as he could and slapped the side of the pool. Simon glanced up and then popped up out of the water, his hair dark and shining like a seal's.

"Well done! There are just a few little details." Then he explained about kicking and the overhead stroke and staying on the surface.

Simon turned and swam back. This time doing it right. Even without a stopwatch or anything, you could tell that he was really fast.

Coach Benjamin hurried up.

"New kid in the neighborhood?" he asked.

"A Simon Robot," said Dad. "Just got him yesterday. You saw how he took that length?"

Coach nodded eagerly.

Although it wasn't official, Dad was a kind of assistant coach. All year he and Coach Benjamin planned and charted and schemed together. And every summer they worked hand in hand to develop a winning team.

"The Viewridge meet is tomorrow," Coach said.

"Last year's champs," said Dad.

"Simon could be a fine addition to the team," said Coach. "What's the rule book say?" he added in a low voice.

"Nothing about robots," said Dad.

"You're putting Simon on the team?" I cried.

"Time to get working," Coach said to me. "Let's try a little harder this year, OK?"

He blew his whistle and set us all on doing our laps. Then he and Dad set to work one-on-one with Simon.

I jumped in and started my laps. Big deal. So Simon beat me once. Beginner's luck. He'd probably be a total loser on the team. Still, maybe I should try to concentrate a little better this year. Maybe if I worked really hard, I could win something.

Then maybe Dad would start looking at me again.

I focused on keeping my breathing regular. One stroke, two strokes. Breathe. One stroke. Two strokes. Breathe. One stroke. It was interesting how the sunlight broke into wavery, shimmering squares on the bottom of the pool. Two strokes. I mean, why squares?

There was a Band-Aid down there. Every week the pool staff collected the Band-Aids that clogged up the pool filter and counted them and then wrote the number on the board. This was supposed to discourage everyone from wearing Band-Aids in the pool, but mostly it made us want to beat last year's number.

"Chip, pick up the pace there!" Prelusky, the real assistant coach, shouted at me.

I kicked harder. Focus. There was another. Focus. Band-Aid. Focus. What if you could make a Band-Aid that looked like a scar? That would be cool. If I had a scar, I'd want one from my ear to the corner of my mouth and then clear across my tongue. Everyone would—

"CHIP!"

Focus.

"Who's the new guy?"

I looked up from where I sat on the grass near the pool. I'd finished my laps, even a bunch extra, but Dad was still working with Simon.

I groaned inside. Mike Neeman stood above me. My nemesis. The guy my dad always compared me to, because Mike's dad, Butch Neeman, was my dad's big rival back when they were kids.

Mike wasn't on the Westerwood swim team. He was on the Viewridge team, but he lived nearby and he hung out at Westerwood a lot, bragging each year about how he was "gonna beat Westerwood's butt." And he usually did, meaning he usually beat *my* butt, since we were in the same age group.

His dad, Butch, was the guy Dad had beaten for the All-City Championship. Now that they're grown-ups, they shake hands after each meet, and Mr. Neeman says things like "good race," "fine effort," and stuff like that, but his beady little eyes say, "My son clobbered your measly son, nah, nah, nah-nah-nah," and his fat, red hand squeezes my dad's hand so hard it makes my dad's eyes water.

"He's a Simon Robot," I said, answering Mike's question about the new guy. "My dad bought him."

"What's your dad doing buying a Simon? Those cost a ton."

"So?" I said.

I didn't mention about Simon being 20 percent off.

"Your dad's a mailman!"

"So?"

"My dad says he's never even been promoted to supervisor."

"So?"

Mike's dad owned the big building-supply store downtown. They got a new media center and a new car practically every year. My dad's car—well, it was better not to think about my dad's car.

Mike shook his head like I was too lame to understand and turned to watch Simon once more.

Simon swam back and forth, back and forth with perfect precision. He could have done it all day.

"He's good," said Mike. Then I could see a thought had struck him. When Neeman has a thought, it's noticeable.

"Hey, I get it! It's in their ads. 'The Perfect Son.' Your dad got a new son. One who can swim."

"He didn't get a new son! He got me a brother. He didn't even know he could swim. He wasn't thinking about that at all."

Mike snorted.

I looked over at my dad, who was practically drooling, he was so excited about Simon's lap times.

"The Perfect Son," Mike repeated thoughtfully. "Guess he doesn't need you anymore, huh?"

That afternoon Mom made me take Simon to summer school with me.

Mom's going to college to learn to be a librarian. A lot of people work on the library computer system, but she wants to work with real books. She even reads real books, the kind where you turn the pages and everything. And she thinks school is superimportant.

"But he knows everything already," I protested.

"Actually," said Simon, discreetly brushing some crumbs off the table that Mom had missed cleaning up, "as I mentioned, we are programmed to learn. Our data banks are not complete. I, for example, have the approximate knowledge of a fifth grader, plus some specialized areas of expertise, of course. Still, there is much that is new to me."

"But I'm doing something with Towler after school," I complained to Mom.

"Who's Towler?" asked Simon.

"My friend," I said. "Best friend," I added, because he was my best friend and he's really cool.

"What's a friend?" asked Simon.

"You don't know what a friend is?!"

Simon quickly scanned his data bank.

"Friend: an ally, a partner, a person whom one knows and is fond of," he recited. "That explains why the concept is not in my top-level data set," he said. "*Fond of* is a feeling, and robots don't have feelings."

"They don't? How weird."

"Feelings are unnecessary to perfect functioning," Simon said stiffly.

Then he announced, "A friend in need is a friend indeed," and started singing a friendship song from his data bank.

"Thank you, Simonson, dear," said Mother. "You can stop now."

I think sometimes he bugged her, too.

She shooed us out the door. "Off you go."

So Simon went to summer school with me.

As we walked up the hill to Bryant Elementary, I asked Simon some more questions.

"OK, so you're kind of like a regular eleven-year-old in the stuff you know?"

"Kind of," said Simon in a way that seemed to say that there was nothing regular about him at all.

"So how about your muscles and eyesight and stuff? I mean do you have, like, superpowers or anything like that?"

"I have the POWER OF DISCIPLINE," he announced. A tiny flare of trumpets sounded from somewhere inside him.

That didn't sound like much of a superpower to me.

"What's that mean?" I said, kind of puffing. The climb up the hill in the summer sun was pretty hot and tiring.

"Well, you'll notice, for example, that unlike you I am having no trouble climbing this hill."

And he wasn't. Simon didn't have a hair out of place, and each step seemed as easy as the one before it.

"That's because, as you will also have noticed, I exercise every morning. And I eat properly and I have a 'can do' attitude. Every day in every way I'm getting better and better."

I stopped and pretended to tie my shoe, but really I was catching my breath.

"My muscles and eyesight and hearing and all my faculties are perfect, of course, but perfect within the realm of human accomplishment. I am what every eleven-year-old boy of good health and good attitude could be, if he, too, had the POWER OF DISCIPLINE."

Trumpet flare.

"How nice," I said.

About as nice as hitting yourself on the head with a little hammer over and over, I thought.

"Well, here we are," I said.

At last we were at Bryant Elementary. Crumbling bricks, sagging portable classrooms in what was once the parking lot, and cracked asphalt in the playground. Just a regular school, but Simon gazed at it with interest.

He flicked through his data banks. "'Hallowed halls of ivy.' 'Institute of higher learning.'" He seemed to be trying to find a match. "'Venerable institution.' Aaah." He seemed to have hit on something. "'Slum,'" he announced.

I started to correct him, but then I spotted Towler. Towler is easy to notice. He's the shortest kid in the school, with bright red hair that sticks out kind of like Einstein's. He's going to summer school this year like me, not because he almost flunked, but because he's in a special computer class. He's supersmart, but he's nice about it. I mean, he never makes me feel dumb. Plus he likes my jokes.

He came up to us, patting his backpack. "I got the stuff. Can you go?"

"Yeah, my mom said OK."

Then he noticed Simon.

"Hey, aren't you a Simonson XX? I saw your ad on TV."

Simon smiled thinly and chimed almost as if he couldn't help it, *"'Extraordinary Products for Ordinary People. DONG!'"*

"You use the new Matrix 3100 SX superprocessor, don't you?"

"Maybe," he said.

"Probably classified information, huh?" said Towler.

"Maybe."

Towler smiled and held out his hand.

"Welcome to humankind," he said. "I come in peace."

"Maybe," said Simon.

"Are you all right?" I asked. I wondered if something had gotten stuck inside him or something.

"I'm fine," he said. "But perhaps we should go to class. With my exceptional powers of observation—although within the range of human capability—I've noticed that everyone has now entered the building."

Simon was right, so we all took off.

"See you later," I called to Towler, who gave me a wave.

Then Simon and I hurried on to class.

Ms. Broadbeam, the vice principal, was the teacher for my summer-school class.

She's not what you would expect from her name. She's tall and thin, with wavery hair. Her voice is kind of like she's singing all the time.

"Good afternoon, class," she warbled as Simon and I slid into our desks. "The word has spread in our little school community, Chip, about your Simonson XX. Perhaps Simonson could tell us a bit about himself?"

Simon stood up crisply.

"He looks so real," Lisa Fox said.

"That's because he is," said Brad Hornbill, who always argued with everyone.

"But he's not really alive," said Lisa.

"Define *alive*," said Brad.

They would have argued a bunch more, but Ms. Broadbeam stopped them and had Simon come to the front of the class to answer questions.

"Are you alive?" asked Brad, first thing.

"I am operational," said Simon.

"Can you die?" asked Brad.

"I can become nonoperational," said Simon.

"Do you care if you're operational or nonoperational?" asked Karen Bingaman, which seemed to get more at the heart of things.

"A robot must protect its own existence," he said, "but if I were nonoperational, I wouldn't know it, so I don't suppose I would care."

"Besides," I added, "robots don't have feelings."

No one paid much attention to me. They wanted to know other things, like what was that thing around his neck (Simon explained it was a bow tie, and Brad Hornbill snickered), and did he eat, and what would happen if his hand got chopped off. Simon said he would have to be returned to the factory for a replacement. I could see him swell up with all the attention and questions, turning this way and that and shooting out his arm to point at some kid with a question. What a show-off!

Everyone wanted to see how smart he was, of course, and Ms. Broadbeam knew that, so the next thing she did was ask Simon to demonstrate some of his knowledge for the class.

"Now them, Simonson," she said. "Can you name the fifty states and their capitals?"

"No," said Simon, "I'm afraid that isn't in my data banks, as yet."

"Oh."

Everyone was disappointed. Even most of us, who had almost flunked fifth grade, knew the state capitals.

"So that you may have the joy of teaching me as if I were a real boy, perhaps you could give me access to the data."

"Here," said Annie Beadle, handing him her social studies book. "The states and stuff are in there."

Simon took the book and quickly flipped through the pages.

"It's the third chapter, I think," said Annie.

"Page fifty-six," said Simon. "And the map on pages

seventy-eight and seventy-nine and then various references in the index, of course, but I won't detail those."

Then he proceeded to name all the states, their capitals, principal exports, and state flowers.

He could have recited the whole book, but Ms. Broadbeam finally stopped him.

"Thank you, Simonson. You are a quick learner, I see. That was a very joyful experience, but now perhaps the best thing would be for you to go over to that corner and read the encyclopedia while the rest of the class reviews their multiplication tables."

The class gave him a polite round of applause, and Simon waved like he was the president boarding a plane, then went over to the bookshelves in the back of the room while we tackled our sevens.

I guess we all looked pretty dumb, the rest of us in the class, I mean. There were about ten of us who had to go to fifth-grade summer school that year. Here we were, already all the way through elementary school, and most of us didn't know our multiplication tables. Simon would have learned them in a second while the rest of us had been trying to learn them since the third grade!

The funny thing is, I didn't feel that dumb. I mean, I guessed I must be dumb, but lots of times my brain seemed to spark along as good as anybody's, but it just couldn't seem to concentrate. Like at the pool, when I was trying to swim laps.

I'd start to learn my sevens, but by about seven times six or so, I'd be wondering what a corn was. I mean, a corn on your foot. You'd see that in books, how somebody had a corn on their toe, but what was that exactly?

"And seven times eight?"

I realized Ms. Broadbeam was asking me.

"Uhmmmm. Seven times eight." I repeated it real slow, trying to add things up in my head.

"Fifty-six," said Ms. Broadbeam in a gentle sing-song. "Seven times eight is fifty-six."

I nodded like she hadn't told me that a million times. I could feel Simon staring at me from the back of the room with his robot eyes.

I hunched my shoulders. Big deal, so I didn't know my multiplication tables. Who cared? I sure didn't. Not at all. Not one bit. Not me. Nope.

I thought I heard Simon snickering his mean little laugh behind me.

Towler was waiting for me on the front steps when school got out. He had a big grin on his face, and right away I felt better.

But then Simon came up.

"Let's go," I said, pushing Towler.

Simon started to follow.

"Go away," I said. "You have to go home."

"What are you and Towler doing?"

"None of your business. Go home."

"Maybe I don't know the way," Simon said.

"Hah! You probably have every step memorized in your data bank, and if you forgot, you could beam up to some satellite and get a map sent to you."

"Maybe."

Towler caught my eye. I could tell he was thinking that maybe Simon could come with us. Then they'd probably spend the whole time talking about computers and stuff.

"Get lost," I said to Simon.

"Why can't I come?"

I thought of the meanest thing I could.

"Because I'm with my friend now, and I don't bring my refrigerator or my vacuum cleaner along when I'm with a friend," I said. "I'm sorry, but I just don't hang out with any of my household appliances."

Simon slowed and stopped.

Towler and I kept walking. I glanced back. Simon looked almost like he was sad, standing there so still with his hands hanging down and his stupid little bow tie poking out under his chin. But then I shook my head. I knew it was just my imagination. Robots didn't have feelings.

Between the Northgate Mall O'Rama and the North-end Mega Mall Plex, there's this strip of asphalt and some dumpsters and stuff, and then behind that are some woods that I guess people forgot about. In the woods, between the tall, old trees, is a trail. It's narrow and rocky and just about not there anymore, but Towler and I discovered it one day, and at the end of the trail is Green Lake. That's what we call it because the water is dark and greenish. It's pretty small, maybe more like a pond, but there's never anybody there except me and Towler, and you can pretend that the sound of the freeway is a stream and you're way out in the wilderness.

Today Towler had this plan. We were going to go fishing. Neither of us had ever been fishing before, so it sounded like a good plan.

He had two poles and some other stuff in his backpack. We took turns carrying the backpack as we started up the trail.

Towler took a deep breath. I did, too, snuffling up the sharp smell of the pine trees.

"Aaaah, wilderness," he said.

"Yeah," I agreed. There was only the faintest whiff of car exhaust.

"Why didn't you want Simon to come?" Towler asked as we walked along.

"He's just a big show-off. He says he's designed to learn things and stuff, but then it takes him a nanosecond to read the whole dictionary. My dad says he's supposed to be an example for me."

I kicked a stone.

"An example? Man, that's bad," said Towler.

"He's even on the swim team now. My dad thinks he's the greatest thing since the remote control."

Towler shook his head. He knows how much my dad likes the swim team and remote controls.

"Next thing, I'll be sleeping in the garage or something. I mean, if we had a garage."

"Maybe you could, like, defeat him at something," said Towler. "Show your dad that he's not so perfect."

"But he *is* perfect."

And I told Towler about his POWER OF DISCIPLINE.

Towler thought it sounded like a really lame superpower, too.

"Still, he's got to have a weakness," said Towler. "Everything has a weakness."

I could tell that Towler was thinking. He likes problems like that.

So while he was distracted, I started to walk just a little bit faster and then faster. Then I started to run, because we always raced at the end to see who could get to the lake first.

"Hey." Towler started running, too, and then he cheated and kept slamming me with the backpack to keep me back. So he won, but he usually does anyway, even if he is so short.

Then we scrambled onto some big sunny boulders and set about figuring out fishing.

Towler had talked to the guy at the sporting goods store, so he showed me how you tie your fishing line to a swivel that clips onto the hook. We clamped some lead weights to our lines, mashed red-pink fish eggs onto our hooks, and dropped our lines into the waters of Green Lake.

Then we waited.

"Maybe there's not any fish in the lake," I said after a while. "It's probably polluted, with the highway nearby."

"No, I've seen them jumping," said Towler.

He leaned back and gazed thoughtfully at the sky.

"What is the POWER OF DISCIPLINE, anyway? I mean, exactly," he said.

"I guess it means he gets up when he's supposed to and exercises and does his homework—not that he ever has any—and cleans his room and puts his clothes away and always eats right. You know, like in the army or something. Only he doesn't have a sergeant guy yelling at him. He does it himself."

Towler nodded. "It's an internal thing, then."

I shrugged. I wasn't sure what Towler was talking about.

We sat there some more.

After a while I said, "Maybe the fish ate our bait. I've read about how that can happen."

We reeled in our lines and checked. The eggs were still there. We tossed out our lines again.

"Maybe you could get the POWER OF DISCIPLINE," said Towler.

"You mean always eating healthy stuff and having combed hair and getting up on time and folding my shirts and stuff? Me?"

Towler looked over at me. He's known me since

preschool. He was reading the letters on the alphabet blocks while I was still trying to eat them.

He sighed. "Yeah, you're right. We better go to Plan B."

"What's that?"

"I don't know yet. I'm working on it," he said.

"What do you do if a fish bites?" I asked.

"The guy at the store said it feels like this little tug, and then you jerk your arms to set the hook." Towler demonstrated. "And then you reel 'em in."

"I think I feel a bite!" I cried.

I jerked and reeled. In came my hook. It was empty. The eggs were gone.

"They ate it!" I said. "There *is* something there."

I rebaited my hook and tossed it in.

Then for a long time we just lay against the warm rocks. Every once in a while I reeled in my hook, and I started to figure out that a lot of things can feel like a tug of a fish, but they aren't.

"Doesn't he ever do anything wrong?" asked Towler.

"Not that I've seen," I said. "Of course he is only two days old."

"Yeah." Towler sat up. "He's like a newborn baby, isn't he?"

I felt another tug. Probably just the pull of a current. My line pulled again and then again. Sharp and hard.

I grabbed my pole and jerked. I could feel something heavy and strong at the other end. My reel started whirring, and faster than I could see, the line went raveling out from it. Whatever was on my line was headed for the middle of the pond!

"Reel him in!" cried Towler. "Reel him in!"

I grabbed the little handle on my reel and started turning.

"My line's going to break!" I said. It stretched like a tight white scar above the water. So I eased off a bit, then reeled a bit, eased off a bit, then reeled. You couldn't go too fast. You couldn't go too slow.

Gradually, I brought the fish in closer.

"There he is," Towler said, pointing.

I could see a dark shadowy shape in the water. It looked big! Like maybe as long as my forearm. The fish flashed near the water's surface, glistening with silver. I pulled him in closer, praying my line didn't snap.

Towler scrambled onto his belly and reached out with a fishing net. I dragged the fish closer. He was as heavy as a hunk of wet cardboard, and my line was so thin and fine, and yet it held. You had to do it just right, I thought. You had to feel the fish through your fingers and arms and the line. Then you could do it.

"Got him!"

Towler pulled the net from the water and onto the boulder. The fish, after all that, just lay there, staring up at the sky with his round wet eye not looking frightened or worried or much of anything. I guess fish don't have much in the way of brains.

"Awesome," said Towler. "You're like a natural or something."

"Well." I shrugged modestly.

We both stood and admired the fish some more, then I carefully worked my hook out of his mouth and untangled his fins from the net. He smelled wet and clean and sort of metallic. Each of his scales was perfect, layered one against the other like tiny silver coins.

I lay on my stomach and lowered my hands into the water. The fish stayed in my hands for just a moment, getting his breath back, I suppose, then he flicked his powerful tail and was gone.

"Cool," I said quietly.

And it was. It was the coolest thing I had ever done.

"I know how we can get Simon," said Towler.

"Cool," I said again, but I was still watching the shadow of my fish.

"I call it Operation Temptation," said Towler. And then he told me all about it.

"I caught a monster fish today," I announced at dinner. "He was this big!"

I held my hands apart.

"Eleven and three-eighteenths inches," said Simon, instantly measuring the gap. "Not even a foot, and, of course, one must make allowances for exaggeration."

If robots had feelings, I'd say Simon was mad at me for not letting him come this afternoon, because if he could be a bigger jerk than he already was, he was being one tonight.

"You caught a fish?" Dad looked up with interest.

"Excuse me, Father," said Simon, turning sideways and blocking me with his back. "I'd like to ask you about my flip turns. I am eager to get it right for tomorrow."

Dad's attention went back to Simon.

"Is Simon racing against Viewridge tomorrow?" I

asked. Coach Benjamin had announced his addition to the team that morning.

Dad nodded.

"He's only been swimming once ever," I protested.

"He did the breast stroke in 36.29," said Dad.

"Chip, why don't you tell us more about your fish?" said Mom.

"I gotta go do Mrs. Cranston's yard now," I said.

"But we want to hear about the fish, don't we, dear?" She looked over at my dad.

"Huh?" he said.

I jumped up and went over to Mrs. Cranston's.

"Good evening, Chip," said Mrs. Cranston, glancing up from her flower bed as I came up the walk.

"'Lo." I scowled. I held out my hand for the dandelion fork.

"Are you all right?" she asked.

I shrugged. What did she care?

"Did something happen today?" She sat back on her heels, looking at me.

"I went fishing," I finally said. "Only nobody cares."

"Oh?"

She sounded kind of interested.

"I caught a fish," I said. "It was pretty big."

"Well!" She sounded kind of impressed.

So I told her all about it. She didn't interrupt me

once to tell me about some time when she went fishing or tell me about how I should try to save the environment or about a better way to fish or anything.

Only at the very end she said, "Was this the first time you went fishing?"

I nodded.

"My," she said.

Then she handed me a trowel. I stared. It wasn't the dandelion fork.

"See those spindly things? Those are weeds. You take that half of the flower bed, and I'll take this side."

I looked at her in surprise. Somehow I had graduated to the flower bed. I took the trowel and attacked the spindly things. We worked for a while in silence, and then I asked, "Have you ever gone fishing?"

"Long ago," she said.

"Did you catch anything?" I asked.

"Not a thing," she said cheerfully.

"Cool," I said. Then I realized that didn't sound very nice.

"Sorry," I said, glancing over at her.

She didn't say anything, but she smiled as she dug into the soil.

Later, as Simon and I got ready for bed, I noticed that Simon didn't play the radio through his mouth like he usually did. He usually insisted on an all-news channel and had numerous comments and opinions on how humans were conducting themselves.

Tonight, he silently and stiffly dusted everything in the room, using a cotton swab to get into all the tight spaces. He acted like my whole room was one big bad smell.

"I guess you're mad at me, huh?" I said.

"Mad?" Simon asked, like he couldn't imagine such a thing. "Hardly. Robots don't have feelings, as you'll recall."

"Well, what *do* you have? I mean, how do you know if you're happy or sad?"

"These words mean nothing to me," said Simon. "Things are either perfect or not perfect."

Suddenly he bent his knees, jumped, and flipped his whole body over so that he landed standing on his hands. He raised his right hand so that he was balanced on only his left hand. A one-handed handstand. He was rock solid, and his face didn't get red or anything.

He began reciting the Gettysburg Address, and when he had finished that, he recited a bunch of facts about the United States. He defined *mulligatawny* and Einstein's cosmological constant, and he ended with, "Seven times eight is fifty-six."

He flipped himself back to his feet, brushed himself off, and announced stiffly, "I'd like to see your refrigerator do *that*."

Swim meets can be pretty confusing if you've never been to one before. There are a lot of races, and things move fast. They do the races one right after the other. And nobody has time for mistakes or messing around.

As Dad tried to start his car the next morning, he explained all this to Simon.

Hrrrrrrrr, hrrrrrrrr. Hrr, hrr scrreeeeeetch, went the car.

"They post the number of the race," said Dad, pumping the gas pedal a few more times. "And the heat, if there is more than one."

Simon nodded.

"Start," Dad said again to the voice-activated ignition panel.

Hrrrrrrr, hrrrrrrr. Screeetch. Wrrrrrrrrrrch.

Dad's car was an early model of the first truly smart

cars. It featured a talking dashboard and windshield wipers that came on automatically when it rained. But, of course, it was secondhand, and Dad had tried to do something tricky with the dashboard voice—change it to sound like him or something—and now it didn't start so good.

"You have to watch for your race because you need to be ready behind the starting block when the time comes. Start!"

Hrrrrrrr, hrrrrrrr. Wrrrrrrrrrrrch. THUNK. Dad gave the dashboard a good whack with the palm of his hand. That sometimes helped.

"Starting block?" asked Simon, sounding a bit uncertain.

"Nothing to it," I said from the backseat. "Piece of cake."

Simon glanced back at me.

I gave him a nice, fake smile.

The starting block is awful—one of the worst parts of a race. It's a little block a few feet high with a slightly sloped top that you dive off to start the race. When the starter tells you, you step up onto it, and when he says, "Take your marks," you bend down, your fingers touching the edge of the block. You try to sort of lean out as far as you can, but the sloped top can be slippery, and you better not fall in because that counts as one false start.

Your head is down and your knees are bent and your muscles want to jump—jump right now! But you have to wait for the buzzer, because if you jump before the buzzer sounds, that's another false start.

Two false starts and you're out. But if you jump too late, well, you lose the race. So what you try to do is to dive at the exact same second the buzzer sounds—like almost before your brain hears it, your muscles hear it, and they spring and you're in the air and you're on your way.

But first you have to wait, bent on the block, every muscle ready, your heart thumping, waiting for the buzzer.

I hate that part.

RRRRR. Rumble, rumble, rumble. PURRRRRRR.

At last the car engine roared to life.

"Here we go!" Dad turned to back out of the driveway. "I think we've really got a chance this year."

"I don't know, Dad. My times haven't been that great," I said.

"Oh, don't worry about that." He looked at Simon. "We've got a few surprises up our sleeve this year."

I was in two races for the Viewridge meet.

My first race was the butterfly. I usually do OK on the butterfly. It's a tricky stroke. Neeman usually comes in first, but I'm a close second place. It was my best bet for beating him, and I'd been practicing hard in the workouts.

Dad gave me a thumbs-up as I climbed onto the block.

It felt like old times, and I smiled.

I looked over at Mike. He seemed a little tense.

"Take your marks," said the starter.

I bent down, and then I don't know what happened. I must have slipped or something. I fell off the block and sank into the pool. I couldn't believe it. I'd never fallen off the block.

I shot up as quickly as I could because I was delaying the whole race. All the other swimmers were on their blocks, shaking out their legs and arms and shooting me angry looks because I'd thrown them off on their timing. All except Neeman, who couldn't have been happier.

I got back up on the block.

"Take your marks," said the starter, sounding annoyed.

I bent down. My legs were shaking and my heart pounded. "Idiot. Idiot. Idiot," it seemed to say. I strained to hear the buzzer over its beat.

Just as it began to beep, I leapt. It was a great start. I was ahead of everyone. I soared up from the depths, ready to swing my arms into the first stroke of the butterfly, and I hit the rope. The false-start rope. Once you begin a race, you can't hear anything underwater, so the way they let you know you jumped the gun is to drop a rope into the water, across the lanes, and it stops the swimmers.

I'd started too soon! My second false start! I was out of the race!

I scrambled out of the water, my face burning hot. Disqualified on my very first race for the season. This had to be a nightmare.

"Jeez, two false starts. I've never seen anyone do that!" I heard Mike's voice cutting through everything.

"Sorry, but you're out of the race," said the starter.

I nodded and, keeping my head down, hurried past my dad and all the other swimmers, into the quiet of the locker room.

I went straight to the showers and stood under the warm water for a long time. I kept swallowing a lump in my throat. I pretended I was a robot and didn't have feelings, and after a while, I felt I could come out of the shower.

When I did, I saw Simon sitting in one corner of the locker room. He was so quiet, it looked like he was turned off, but he sort of clicked on when I came in.

"How'd you do?" he asked.

I didn't answer.

I went around the bank of lockers and sat in the corner on the other side.

"Are you all right?" he asked.

"Go stick your finger in a light socket," I said.

There was a moment's silence, and then he said, "Seven times eight is fifty-six."

"Shut up!" I cried.

I could hear him turn himself off. There was something very satisfied about his CLICK!

The freestyle relay was the last race of the day and Westerwood's last hope. Despite my screwup, the team had done pretty good, and we actually had a chance of winning our first meet of the year. Everyone was excited. But we had to win the freestyle relay.

In a relay, four swimmers make up a team. When one guy finishes his part of the race, the next guy dives in. It's called a freestyle because supposedly you can use any swim stroke you want, including the backstroke, breaststroke, or the butterfly—but I've never seen anyone do anything but the crawl.

The team was me, Steve Dori, Randy Small, and Simon. Dad and Coach Benjamin had been saving him all afternoon, just for this race.

As I made my way to the swimmers' waiting area, Mike Neeman brushed past.

"Hey, Rope-a-Dope," he said. Several nearby kids snickered. "Nice job of beating my butt."

I tried to think of something really smart to say back, only I couldn't. Fortunately, just then, Simon made his entrance, and everyone stopped talking to stare.

It was the first time the crowd had seen him. Everyone was interested in the robot that could swim, of course, and Simon made the most of it. He strode slowly out of the locker room and paused, framed by the doorway.

He looked incredible. His skin gleamed with a golden tan, and his muscles were buff. Like he'd worked out in a gym for years.

He walked slowly and magnificently toward the starting area. Not a hair was out of place. He smiled, and a ray of sunlight glinted off his perfect white teeth. How did he do that?

"Oooh," said the crowd.

"Where'd you get that tan?" I said.

"One of the advantages of synthetic melanin," he said, rather smugly.

"You did something to your muscles, too," I said.

"They are not really stronger than they ever were. That would be an unfair advantage. My synthetic fibers have a strength that is available to any eleven-year-old who happens to be in prime physical shape

But I can give them a temporary look of enlargement. A psychological advantage that I'm not ashamed to take advantage of."

"Cool," said Randy. Steve Dori nodded his head excitedly. They were pumped and ready to take on Viewridge, and they were thrilled to have Simon on our side.

"OK," said Coach Benjamin. "Here's what we're going to do. Chip, you're going to be leadoff. Then Steve. Then Randy. And Simon, you'll handle that last lap."

Dad hovered nearby.

"Ready, Simon?" he said.

Simon saluted.

Dad glanced at me.

"Don't fall off," he said.

"Swimmers, take your marks." The starter raised his gun.

I bent down and rested my fingers on the edge of the block. For just a second I felt myself teetering. If I fell in again, I would never come up. I'd rather drown.

I steadied myself, straining to hear the beep of the starting gun.

"Rope-a-Dope." I heard a voice behind me.

It was Neeman. He was the last swimmer for the Viewridge relay team. He was back behind the timers, waiting with the rest of the teams, but his voice carried and blended into the sound of the buzzer.

The buzzer. The buzzer! Oh, no! The buzzer had gone off! I pushed off as hard as I could and hit the water cleanly and smoothly. But it was too late. It was much too late. I'd gotten an incredibly slow start.

The other swimmers were already several strokes ahead of me. I swam as hard as I could, reached the far edge of the pool and flipped underwater, making my turn, pushing off that end. It was a good turn, but it didn't make any difference.

The lead swimmer on Viewridge's number-one team was half a pool length ahead of me. And the other four teams were staggered along behind him. I was dead last. By the time I touched the edge of the pool and Steve dove in, everyone's second swimmer was already gone.

I was too sick even to go to the locker room. I just stood at the side and stared in horror.

Steve and Randy swam as hard as they could, and they gained a couple of places, but we were still in third place—far behind Viewridge's leading team—when Simon climbed onto the starting block.

The crowd turned to him. He looked calm and confident. As Randy neared the end of his lap, Simon bent forward into the dive position.

At the exact nanosecond that Randy's fingers touched the pool edge, Simon dove. A perfect dive. He skimmed into the water at a flat, fast angle and came shooting to the surface, ready to begin his stroke.

But something went horribly wrong.

"Oh, no!" shrieked Randy. "He's got the wrong stroke."

Simon was doing the breaststroke!

The crowd groaned in disbelief. Even though in theory you could use any stroke in the freestyle, no one ever did—they were all too slow compared to the crawl. Simon could never win using the breaststroke.

Everyone turned to look at my dad and Coach Benjamin. But they didn't look the least bit worried. In fact, they smiled. This is exactly what they had planned!

Everyone turned to look back at Simon. His arms moved with the relentless precision of a machine. With each stroke he shot forward as clean and sleek as a seal, a calm smile on his face. He passed swimmer after swimmer, and by the the time he reached the end of the pool and flipped to turn back for the last lap, only Mike Neeman was ahead of him.

Neeman's arms plowed into the water. He kicked frantically. He was swimming for all he was worth, but Simon stroked relentlessly on. He caught up with Mike. For a moment they were dead even, then Simon calmly took the lead.

Simon's hands hit the end of the pool two full strokes ahead of Mike.

Simon had won! Westerwood had won the meet. Our first victory over Viewridge in years!

Mr. Neeman hopped up and down, shouting, "But he can't do that. He did the breaststroke! He has to do the crawl!"

"It's called the freestyle, not the crawl," crowed Dad. "He can use any stroke he wants. Check the rule book."

"But, but . . ." Mr. Neeman shook his fists and jumped up and down some more. He couldn't believe it. He didn't want to believe it, but my dad was right.

Mr. Neeman thought of something else.

"He's a robot. You can't use robots. They have to be human!"

"Check the rule book," said Coach Benjamin. "It doesn't say anything about humans."

He and Dad high-fived each other. They had figured it all out.

The crowd surged around my dad, shaking his hand and slapping him on the back while Simon stood modestly by his side.

"I can't believe it, not after that dreadful start," someone said.

"Hip hip hooray!" a lady shouted, and the Westerwood crowd took it up. "Hip hip hooray!"

"That's quite a boy you got there," said Steve's dad.

"Good job, son," said Dad, clapping Simon on the back.

I quickly walked away. I didn't shower or anything. I pulled on a T-shirt, grabbed my gym bag, and by the time I got to the gate, I was running. Running, running, running.

I didn't stop until I got home. Then I went into the bathroom and threw up.

"It's time for Operation Temptation," I said to Towler over the phone.

"I know you're in there," said Dad, knocking loudly on the door to my room.

I'd heard Dad and Simon come home earlier, bursting with excitement over the meet. Mom got home from school, and I could hear Dad telling her all about it. Probably she's the one who noticed I wasn't around.

So then Dad knocked on my door. And gradually it became clear that I wasn't coming out. Dad tried being understanding. He tried being mad. He bribed. He threatened.

From the murmuring voices, I could tell that he and Mom and Simon were now all huddled out in the hall, planning their next move.

"So are you ready?" I said to Towler.

"How much junk food do you have in the house?" Towler asked.

Mom and Dad were still worriedly consulting when a few minutes later I threw open the door to my room and greeted them all with a big smile.

"Now, Chip," said Dad. "Everyone makes mistakes."

"I'm sorry it was such a bad day," said Mom.

"I broke the club record for the breaststroke," said Simon.

"Oh hush!" Mother cried. Even Dad frowned.

"It's all right," I said. "You know, maybe my attitude hasn't been good."

"What?" said Dad, who was in the middle of telling me about how you had to keep on trying.

"Maybe I've been unfair to Simon."

Mom and Dad looked kind of astonished.

"Maybe it's time I took advantage of this great opportunity to learn from this wonderful role model you and Mom have provided for me." Just what Towler had told me to say.

I thrust out my hand toward Simon. "Congratulations, brother, on your wonderful win today."

He hesitated before holding out his hand.

"Thanks . . . brother," he said cautiously.

I shook his hand in a good, firm way.

"I, ah, I'm very impressed, Chip," said Dad.

Mom nodded, although I could tell she wasn't completely convinced.

Still, she went off to cook a celebration dinner of creamed chip beef, and I listened to Simon's pre-dinner lecture on presidential inaugural speeches like he was the most fascinating thing in the world. After dinner we all sat down to a game of cards.

A lot of people use electronic gaming screens these days, but Mom likes real cards. Paper cards. It's kind of funny how both my parents still work with paper—Mom with her real books and Dad carrying mail for the Post Office. Of course, Dad says he hasn't seen an actual, personal letter in ages—that's all done by e-messaging. All he hauls around is junk mail, but it's still paper.

"And darn heavy, too," he says proudly.

"What should we play?" Mom said, shuffling the cards with a snap.

"Bridge," said Dad.

"Pinochle," I said.

Simon was scanning as fast as he could, trying to learn the rules.

"Wait," he cried. "I think I've got it."

"Don't sweat it," I said. "We don't know how to play those anyway."

"It's just a joke," said Dad.

"We always play the same thing," said Mom, starting to deal out the cards. "Crazy Eights."

"Only we make it Crazy Threes," I said.

"We're missing the three of spades, so if I deal you

a card short, you get to play with an invisible three of spades," explained Mom.

"Of course, it's not really invisible because everyone knows you have it, since you're short a card," added Dad.

Simon blinked.

Mom, Dad, and I started giggling. Not at Simon, at ourselves.

"But that's not logical," Simon protested.

"It's OK," I said. "It's just a family thing."

And, watching Mom laughing and Dad's grin, I felt really good saying that.

I looked over at Simon. It was weird. He was eagerly glancing back and forth between Mom and Dad with his mouth open like he was trying to laugh, but couldn't. Maybe his laugh options only included that one mean laugh, but it sure looked like he was trying for a real laugh, only I guess he didn't know how.

And for a moment, I almost felt sorry for him. I almost felt bad about what Towler and I had planned—but not that bad.

Later I lay in my bunk, staring up into the darkness. I kept seeing myself fall off the starting block over and over, wishing I could catch myself, wishing I could turn everything into reverse, like playing a video backward.

Simon's voice came drifting down from the bunk above.

"Chip, are you awake?"

"No."

"Oh."

I could sense Simon's thoughts whirring. Then it hit him, and he said in an annoyed tone, "Yes, you are. Logically you have to be, or you couldn't have answered me."

"OK. What do you want?" I said. It suddenly occurred to me that robots were awful stuck on being logical.

"What's more important, a brother or a friend?"

I thought about it for a while.

"That's a hard question," I finally said.

"Well, which do you like more?"

"A friend you choose to like. A brother—well, I guess you're supposed to like them no matter what."

"But you don't always?"

I didn't answer, but it was pretty clear what my answer was.

"Oh," said Simon.

"But they're important?" Simon asked after a while. "A brother is important?"

"Yes," I said.

"I thought so," he said with a kind of quiet pleasure. Then he added, "Would you like some nice music? It helps humans to sleep, I understand."

"No," I said. "I don't need any help getting to sleep."

"OK." Simon sighed and clicked himself off.

I tossed and turned all night, thinking about all the people crowded around my dad after the race, telling him what a great son he had. But they didn't mean me.

The next afternoon after summer school, Towler came home with Simon and me.

"Why's he coming to our house?" asked Simon. "He should go to his own house."

"We're going to hang out," I said.

"*Hang out.*" Simon scanned his data banks. "*Slang term for being with someone, usually a friend.*"

"I guess you probably don't want me around then," he added stiffly.

"Oh, no," I said. "We want you to hang with us, honest."

"Really?"

Towler nodded.

"You do?! Swell! Er, I mean, cool," he said.

He turned to Towler.

"I can change my hair color. Want to see?"

And he turned it bright orange with black stripes.

"Do you use the new Chameleon Chromlux gel?" Towler asked.

"That's old stuff."

"Really?" Towler was thrilled to be getting the inside news.

"There's this new technique," Simon said, lowering his voice.

"Hey, I'll race you," I said to Towler.

I slammed him with my backpack and took off. Towler took off after me, and after a second, so did Simon.

Sometimes I have a nightmare. In my nightmare, a thing is chasing me. Maybe a machine, maybe a wolf, maybe a man. But they all run like Simon. Steady and relentless, until they get you. Simon passed Towler. Simon passed me. Simon was so far ahead of us that Towler and I stopped running and walked the rest of the way home, breathing hard.

"Two point three minutes and twelve nanoseconds," Simon announced as we came up the front walk. "Versus three point eight minutes and fifty nanos. I win."

"You always do," I said. "Come on. Let's all go to the family room."

Towler and I plopped down on the brown fake-leather couch. Simon wasn't quite sure what to do. He stood there like a floor lamp.

Towler clicked on the media center. Even though it's old, it has a screen that covers one whole wall and four Gutblast Surround Sound speakers in each corner.

Towler flicked through a couple hundred channels on the remote.

Simon stared at the screen. He'd never watched the media center before. We had been too busy with lessons on inaugural speeches, and swimming, and school and stuff. His eyes jerked back and forth, trying to keep up with the changing images.

"All right!" exclaimed Towler, coming to a halt on the Universal Music Channel.

The Most Awesome Battle of the Bands in Galactic History was on. Supposedly, it was the biggest nonstop rock event ever. It had been going on for over a month, and they were down to the last day and the finalist bands.

The Decibels from Hell was on center stage. Towler sent the volume to the top of the scale.

"Awesome speakers!" he screamed as we were blasted back in our seats.

Staring at the screen, Simon stumbled backward into Dad's recliner–massage chair. Towler and I sneaked a glance his way.

All the signs of instant addiction were there. His eyes never left the screen, and his blink rate practically stopped. He began to breathe in time with the music.

"All right!" Towler yelled in my ear. "Time for snacks."

Simon didn't even notice when we got up and went into the kitchen. We loaded up. Four six-packs of

Orangey Eco-Pop, a megabag of potato chips, a huge box of Lot-o-Choca Choc-o-lot-a Cookies, three pudding snacks, monster cheese puffs, genuine imitation fried pork rinds, beef jerky bits in the giant economy pack, and a jumbo can of whipped cream.

We set it on the coffee table in the family room. Towler cracked open a can of pop and casually, ever so casually, handed it over to Simon.

"Thirsty?"

Simon never took his eyes off the screen. He simply held his hand out, and Towler gave him the can. Simon closed his fingers around it. He brought it to his lips. He took a sip.

He paused for a moment, glanced at the can, a bit puzzled. Orangey Eco-Pop had enough sugar in it to clog up a horse. We held our breaths. The Decibels from Hell screamed out something like "Rotten scum of an Englishmun," and Simon's attention snapped back to the media center. He took a big gulp of his Orangey Eco-Pop and then another gulp. Then he drained it. He crushed the can into a little, flat circle, dropped it on the floor beside him, and held out his hand for another.

Towler and I settled back. Simon was hooked.

After that it was just a matter of handing him things. Slowly but surely he ate his way through the megabag of chips, the cookies, the pudding snacks, the cheese puffs, the giant economy pack of beef jerky bits, and the genuine imitation pork rinds.

Slowly but surely, he slumped lower and lower in the chair, crumpled snack bags and flattened pop cans heaped around him. His face was crusted with crumbs and dribbled pop. His bow tie was sideways. His mouth hung open, drooling. He looked like he couldn't think his way out of a paper bag. He was disgusting!

Over the roar of the media center, I heard the sound of my mom coming in.

"We're in here," I yelled. Like she could miss the howls of the latest band, Puke.

I saw her in the doorway staring at Simon. She looked pale. She turned and yelled something. My dad must have just come in.

"Now!" I screamed at Towler.

And Towler put the jumbo can of whipped cream into Simon's hand.

My dad got to the door just in time to see Simon, sprawled on the chair, his glazed eyes fixed on the media center, his head half-thrown back, his mouth flung open, squirting whipped cream down his throat till it mounded over his lips like an erupting volcano and cascaded down the sides of his mouth in a disgusting avalanche of drool and sugar to join the crumbs and torn wrappers and sticky, crushed pop cans heaped about him. He squirted till the entire contents of the jumbo can of whipped cream was heaped in his mouth, then he sucked it all in one humongous slurp. He let out a massive burp and heaved the empty can at the screen.

The whipped-cream can hit the media center, ricocheted off the screen, and smashed into IT—Dad's giant silver trophy. The trophy toppled from its shelf, hitting the linoleum floor with a sickening clang.

"Stink," shrieked Puke. "YOU STINK!!"

Dad strode to the media center and slammed it off.

And then it was really, really quiet.

He looked at his trophy on the floor. He looked at Simon.

Simon started blinking fast. He sat up. He looked at the hideous mess surrounding him. He stared at the trophy on the floor and tottered to his feet

I quickly scooped up the trophy before Simon accidentally stepped on it.

"I can explain, sir," Simon said hastily.

I handed Dad his trophy.

"It's very simple." Simon quickly straightened his bow tie and slicked back his hair. "Chip made me do it."

I looked shocked. Towler looked shocked. Clearly the mess was all Simon's. I didn't have a crumb on me. Simon had thrown the whipped-cream can. Simon had knocked over the trophy. My face had a sad, noble kind of look. Like I couldn't believe how low some things could sink.

"I'm very disappointed, Simon!" Dad said, his face a furious red. "I expected more of a Cyborg Corporation product."

"But sir," protested Simon.

"That's enough!" he snapped. "I expect this mess to be cleaned up, and then you may go to your room!"

"Yes, sir." Simon quickly bent down and began to pick up.

"Should I help Simon?" I asked, being even more noble.

Mom looked kind of suspicious. Maybe I'd gone too far.

"This is Simon's mess," announced Dad. "But it was big of you to offer, Chip."

He clapped me on the back, and we all left Simon to do his chore.

Later, when I came into my room, Simon sat stiffly in the desk chair.

"You tricked me," he said. "You just pretended you wanted to hang out with me."

"It's easy to be good when nothing tempts you," I said, repeating what Towler said when he explained Operation Temptation to me. "We were testing your POWER OF DISCIPLINE."

"Well, thank you," he said. His trumpet flare sounded defiant.

I blinked.

"I am now stronger and better than ever," Simon announced. "Every day in every way I am getting better and better. So, thank you."

Then he smiled. I'd begun to notice that it was never good when Simon smiled.

Simon didn't say a word to me the next morning. He didn't tell me to get up, or advise me to exercise, or sneer about waste products.

At swim practice, he worked like the machine he was and listened and nodded to every word Coach Benjamin and Dad said. I could see Dad pretty quickly forgetting about the mess from yesterday.

I went to the lane the farthest away from them and sort of paddled back and forth. After what had happened at the swim meet, it was hard to put much heart into it.

Dad noticed and scowled at me, so I thrashed just a bit harder, but really, what was the point?

At class in school, Simon helped Ms. Broadbeam correct some papers. And before and after class, he dazzled everyone by doing about a hundred back flips in a row while playing a local rock station through his mouth.

At home, he cleaned the whole house and popped in a pot roast for dinner. Mom, coming home worn out from her librarian class, practically had tears in her eyes, she was so pleased.

I quickly called Towler. "He's stronger than ever!"

"I've been doing some research on the Simonson XX," he said. "I got another idea, but we have to catch Simon when he's asleep."

I asked Mom if Towler could spend the night.

"He's going to camp in a couple of days," I reminded her, "and we want to try out his new tent."

Towler and I set up his tent in my backyard, arranged our sleeping bags, and crawled in for the night. Simon acted like he wasn't interested in us, but I noticed the curtain in my bedroom window quickly drop when I looked that way.

I was dreaming of wolves in a circle around me, licking their lips, when Towler's watch beeped. It was two in the morning.

We wriggled out of our sleeping bags and crept across the dark lawn. I opened the back door carefully, and we slipped down the hall to my room. I carefully creaked open the door.

A faint light spilled into the room from the hall. Just enough to see Simon lying stiff and still on the top bunk. We were in luck. His right leg was outside his blanket, and his heel was just over the edge of the mattress. It was his right heel we wanted.

"There's a control panel there," Towler had explained earlier.

Towler nudged me and nodded toward Simon's heel. I swallowed, reached out, and took it in my hands.

Simon whirred faintly, then quieted again.

It was creepy fiddling around with Simon's heel. His skin was pretty much like regular skin, but it moved around on his "bones" kind of like a plastic bag. I mooshed it back and forth, trying to see if I could get the panel door to slide open. Then I started poking at the heel bones. Maybe there was a button or something. Finally, I took a deep breath and gave the bottom of his heel a sharp little rap with my hand.

With a quiet click, the back of Simon's heel slid open to reveal a small panel with blinking green lights.

Towler stepped forward. He had a tiny screwdriver that he used to work on his computer. He carefully turned the adjustment screw on the panel.

Nothing happened.

"Turn it a little more," I whispered.

Towler gave it a twist.

Nothing happened.

"More."

Towler wrenched the thing, and the lights on Simon's control panel blazed red.

"Stand back!" Towler cried.

Simon sat bolt upright. A honking voice blared from his ears.

"Warning. Warning. Warning."

He swung his legs over the side of the bed and slid to the floor. He tottered for a moment, then lurched forward. His arms stretched out in front of him like Frankenstein's monster.

"Warning. Warning. Warning."

Simon slammed out the bedroom door and down the hall. He turned and smashed into the wall. Turned the opposite way and smashed into that wall. He turned again and came straight toward me and Towler.

His eyes were wide. He stared right at me, but he didn't really see. His hands stretched toward us like hooks, and he just kept on coming.

"Run!" Towler screamed.

Dad stormed out of his bedroom, pulling on his undershorts.

"Simon's gone crazy," I cried, darting past him.

"Warning. Warning. Warning."

Dad took one look and leapt on Simon, slamming him to the floor. His legs kept moving as if he was walking, but he was on his back. It was all Dad could do to hold him down.

"Warning. Warning. Warning."

Mom came running out.

"His leg!" Dad cried.

Mom grabbed Simon's right leg and hung on for life.

"The reset button," yelled Dad.

Mom yanked a hairpin from her hair and just started jabbing at the control panel. She must have hit something, because suddenly the warning noise stopped and Simon froze in place. He stared calmly at the ceiling.

Dad lay gasping across his chest. After a moment, he wheezed, "Simon?"

Simon lowered his legs and nodded.

"Yes, sir," he said. "Sorry, sir. I'm all right now."

Dad and Mom both sat up.

"What happened?" said Dad.

"My memory bank informs me that there was an unauthorized adjustment to my activation panel."

"Unauthorized?" Dad's head swung our way.

Me and Towler stood a little way down the hall, our eyes wide, still half ready to run.

"I don't know what he's talking about," I started to say, but then I saw Dad's eye fall on Towler's hand and the tiny screwdriver he still held.

Dad rose from the floor like a tidal wave.

"What do you think you're doing?" he roared.

"I can explain, Dad." Only of course I couldn't, but it didn't matter.

"Do you have any idea what a Simonson XX costs?"

Towler probably did, but I don't think Dad really wanted an answer.

"This is the last straw! Ever since we brought Simon into this house, you have resisted, you have fought, you have complained. You aren't learning a thing! And now you're trying to destroy him!"

"He doesn't belong here!" I suddenly shouted back. "You say it's for me, but it's not. You just want a winner is all. All you care about is winning."

"And you don't care about anything." Dad's voice got quiet, but hard. "You're flunking school. You mess around at swim practice. You don't even try."

I swallowed. I did try . . . sort of. I did care. But Dad would never understand how I just couldn't seem to make it work. How it all just fell apart on me no matter how good I wanted to be.

So that's when I shouted back, "That's right! I don't care. I don't care about Simon and his example. I don't care about school. And I sure don't care about your stupid old swim team. In fact, I quit!"

"Fine!" yelled Dad. "That's fine with me. Now I can concentrate on Simon."

"That's all you do, anyway!" I screamed.

Dad and I stood staring at each other, breathing hard.

And then after that there was nothing much to say.

"Everyone's pretty upset right now," Mom said, looking pretty upset herself. "Let's go back to bed. Let's all get a good night's sleep, and things will look better in the morning."

So we all slumped back to our beds.

"I'm sorry," said Towler over and over.

"Forget it," I said. "I'm glad. I'm thrilled. I'm ecstatic."

"Right," said Towler.

But I don't think anyone had a good night's sleep, and nothing looked better in the morning.

The next morning, I heard Dad and Simon leaving in the car for swim practice.

"Start!" I heard Dad yelling at it. He sounded madder at it than ever.

Pretty soon after that we took down the tent, and Towler, after apologizing again for about the millionth time, finally left.

Mom came to hug me good-bye before she went to school.

"I'm sorry things got so angry last night," she said.

I shrugged.

She sighed and patted me on the arm.

"Give it a few days. Your dad will cool down. Maybe you'll feel like going back on the team."

"I'm never going back," I said. "I quit."

"You might change your mind. Don't quit. At least stay on the team roster," she urged.

I shrugged. What did it matter?

With a last worried look, Mom hurried off to catch her bus.

I wandered about the house like a bum. I scratched my belly, cracked open a root beer, and slopped it down.

I looked out the window and saw old Mrs. Cranston out in her garden. I hadn't been over in a couple of days, and I was supposed to go every day.

"Well, who cares," I said to myself. I wasn't going to swim another lap this summer, and I wasn't going to pull another dandelion. I'd had it.

I went to the family room and turned on the media center. I didn't even bother to look up when Simon peeked in after swim practice. He glanced at the screen. His eyes started flicking back and forth. He turned kind of pale and quickly left the room.

He tried to talk to me on our way to Bryant that afternoon, but after a while he gave up. I had nothing to say to him.

In class, when Ms. Broadbeam asked what seven times eight was, I answered "seventy-eight," just like Brad Hornbill always did. It was easier than trying to figure it out.

On the way home from school, Simon tried doing handstands and flips and things to get my attention.

"Just leave me alone," I said. "Leave me very, very alone."

• • •

The next day, just before Dad and Simon left for practice, Dad came and stood in the doorway to my room.

"Now Chip," he said, clearing his throat. "Winners never quit, and quitters never win."

"Well, I never win, so I quit," I said.

He turned and left.

I slept in again. When I got up, I thought about calling Towler. Then I remembered he was at camp for three weeks. I watched the media center for a while. Clicked it off and peered next door, wondering where Mrs. Cranston was. Her car was gone.

Darn! And I really wanted to weed. That's when I realized I might actually die of boredom.

I went to my room and loaded up my backpack.

Half an hour later I was headed up the path to Green Lake. My fishing pole was in my pack, and I carried a plastic bucket with some worms and fishing stuff in it. I whistled a little tune like I was really happy. But it wasn't the same without Towler.

I whistled a little louder. The trail was so quiet and still. The sunlight made bright slabs between the dark shadows of the trees. Dark and light, dark and light. I walked up the trail a little faster.

I heard a twig snap.

I paused and listened hard. All I could hear was

my own breathing. I hurried up the path. I hurried a little faster. I ran like mad. I felt better when I burst out into the sunny clearing around the lake.

I sat on the flat boulders and put my rod together, fixed the line, and baited the hook. I dropped it into the water with a satisfying *plop*.

This was more like it. I lay back on the warm, flat rocks.

Slowly, I became aware of the creepy feeling that someone was watching me.

I sat up and looked around.

Something flickered near the trail.

"Who's there?" I said. "I know karate," I added, even though I don't.

A head peeked out from behind a tree.

It was Simon!

"What are you doing here?"

Simon stepped closer.

"I followed you. I saw you just as Dad dropped me off, and I followed."

I couldn't believe it. He was dressed in his nice slacks and brown shoes and bow tie. He looked unbelievably stupid out here in the woods.

"What are you doing?" He stepped closer.

"I'm getting away from stupid robots!"

Simon came closer and sat on the very edge of one of the boulders.

I turned back to my fishing in disgust. It was quiet

for a bit, then he said, "According to my data bank, you would have better luck casting your line in the shadows, where the fish congregate in the heat of the day."

I threw down my fishing pole.

"Put 'em up!" I cried, raising my fists.

"What are you doing?" Simon backed up in alarm.

"You want to fight? I'll show you a fight."

"But I don't want to fight."

I swung at him, but Simon just stood there.

"Come on, you big chicken."

"I can't," he said.

"You mean you won't!" I said. "You're just a big fat chicken. *Bruuck. Brruuuck!* Chicken, chicken, chicken."

I danced around him.

"I can't. It's in the laws."

"What laws?"

"The Three Laws of Robotics. They are the three laws that govern every robot."

"What a lame excuse!"

"No, it's true. A famous writer, Isaac Asimov, formulated them in the latter half of the twentieth century."

Simon began to list them.

"Number one: A robot may not injure a human being or, through inaction, allow a human being to come to harm. Number two: A robot must obey the orders given it by human beings, except where such orders would conflict with the first law. Number three: A robot must protect its own existence, as long as such protection does not conflict with the first or second law.

"So, as you can see, I can't fight you. It's law number one."

"Well, law number two states you have to obey my orders, and I order you to fight me."

"Law number one is stronger than law number two."

"Law number three says you have to protect yourself. What if I just punched you right now!?"

"Go on," he said. "Hit me in the stomach."

"All right. I will."

And then I proceeded to punch him a bunch of times. It was like hitting a punching bag, only one that talked.

"That was a force two point five hit with a slight deflection to the right of the lower abdominus," he said. He was analyzing every punch!

"You're losing force," he said. "That was only a one point eight impact."

I took a wild swing at his jaw.

"Ouch!! What's in there!?" I cried, shaking my hand and dancing around.

"Titanium," he said proudly. He brushed a bit of dust off his slacks. I hadn't fazed him one bit.

Suddenly I sagged, all the anger fizzling out of me like a balloon sputtering to the ground.

"Oh, what's the use," I said. "You're perfect. No wonder my dad likes you better."

I picked up my fishing gear.

"Where are you going?"

"Home," I said, and started walking away. "You might as well have my fishing hole, too."

"But, but wait," Simon said. "I have something to say."

I shrugged and kept on walking.

"Please." The word came out of Simon's mouth like his throat was rusted. I'd never heard him say "please" before, which was kind of odd now that I thought about it. Being the "Perfect Son" and all.

"What is it?" I sighed, turning around to face him.

Simon cleared his throat, pulled at his bow tie, and finally said, "You may recall that I was twenty percent off?"

I nodded. I wasn't really very interested.

"Well, it seems that I am not one hundred percent perfect."

"What?"

"I'm ninety-nine point nine percent perfect, mind you. But still"—he paused and swallowed—"there is a flaw."

"A flaw?"

"It seems," he stammered, "it seems that I have, well, *feelings*."

"Feelings? You mean like humans?"

Simon's head sagged in shame.

"I find that I have these odd sensations inside at times. It's most unusual. A 'crinkly' thing near my stomach, and sometimes something that tugs at my mouth as if—as if it might smile," he ended in a stricken whisper.

"Well, you do have that mean laugh," I said.

"Yes, well, in truth that was laughing *at* you, not *with* you. This is different. I've studied all the literature and all that. And I find that these sensations mean that I'm fond of you. I find that I would like to be your friend."

"What?!"

"Friend: a person whom one knows well and—"

"I know what a friend is!" I cried. Friends? With Simon?

"No way!" I said fiercely. "When the Earth is a blackened cinder adrift in endless space."

"Oh." Simon swallowed.

"I—I find that I have this tight sensation in my throat," he said after a moment. "It hurts when I swallow, and my eyes have a burning sensation. I wonder what that is."

He blinked rapidly.

I sighed. I knew all about that feeling.

"It means you're sad," I said. "It means your feelings are hurt."

"Oh, I didn't know feelings could get hurt." Simon actually perked up a bit at this information. He liked learning facts. "Not only do I have feelings, but things can happen to them. How interesting.

"So what do you say . . . pal?" He said the word *pal* like he was trying on a new shoe.

"No!" I said.

"I've never had a friend before." There was a little quiver in his voice.

"No!"

"Please." Again with the rusty throat, and now it looked like a tear glistened in his eye.

"Aaargghhh!!" I shook my arms in frustration. He looked at me like a sad puppy waiting to be adopted at the pound. It wasn't fair!

"Oh, all right!" I finally cried. "Maybe for an hour we can try it, but only if you don't call me 'pal.'"

"OK," he said excitedly. And then he added shyly, "buddy."

I rolled my eyes.

Then something funny happened to his mouth. The sides turned up. I realized he was smiling. Not like his perfect smile with the perfect teeth. This was kind of a shy smile. A nice smile.

Man, I didn't want him to turn out to be nice, too.

After a moment he said, "Now what do we do? I mean, now that we're friends. What do friends do?"

It was hard to explain. Finally I said, "Well, you just do stuff together."

Simon nodded crisply. "Perhaps we could fish."

I shook my head. Nothing was biting. Simon was right—it was probably too hot.

"Let's go swimming," I said. "I'm boiling."

I pulled off my T-shirt. Simon carefully undid his bow tie and unbuttoned his shirt. I took off my pants and underpants.

He hesitated. "Is it proper to be naked?"

"No."

I ran into the pond. The bottom was mucky and soft, but the water was clear.

Simon pulled off his pants and his briefs and made a careful stack of his clothes. I was interested to see that he was built like a regular human boy in every way.

He walked out into the pond till he was next to me.

"How many laps should we do?" he said.

"Laps?" I said. "Why would we do laps?"

"Aren't we swimming?"

"Swimming isn't laps. I mean, not this kind of swimming."

"Oh! What's it for, then?"

"It's not for anything. It's just for fun."

"Fun?" Simon started scanning his data banks.

"Don't worry," I said. "You'll know it when you feel it."

Then I splashed him. He splashed me back. We both dug in with our hands and heaved up huge fountains of water at each other.

"I think I feel it!" Simon cried, water streaming down his face.

I took off for the other side of the pond.

It took him a moment to realize that I was racing him to the other side, but soon I heard the steady splash of his perfect breaststroke behind me. I dug in, but even with a head start, he beat me. He slapped the side of a log sticking out from shore and declared, "Forty point six seconds."

Then he looked worried. "Is that OK? To win, I mean? I mean, for friends?"

"Hey, I'll never swim like you," I admitted.

"You could," Simon said. "I could teach you. It's really just a matter of working a little bit each day. That's the real secret to the POWER OF DISCIPLINE."

There was that tiny trumpet flare again.

"No thanks, Simon."

I lay on my back. The sun was warm on my face. I floated in lazy circles.

Simon flipped onto his back and lay there, too. He kept looking over at me and smiling eagerly. He was so happy to be friends, it was hard to keep hating him.

"What's it like to be you?" he suddenly said.

"To be me?"

"I mean, what does it feel like? I understand that each human feels a bit different inside from every other human being. I'm trying to understand human feelings. Perhaps my flaw could be the basis of an interesting research project," he added.

What did it feel like to be me? Nobody had ever asked me that before. I thought for a long time.

"Twenty lashes with a wet noodle," I finally said.

I could sense Simon whirring through his data banks. He'd probably never heard that expression before, but my dad had said it once. Pretending to be mad one time, he had said, "You will have to have twenty lashes with a wet noodle." And I suddenly realized that was what being me was like.

"When you're like me," I said, "it's like you get lashed all day long, only in a soggy kind of way. You get so you practically don't notice anymore.

"Don't know the answer to the question in school. *Lash*. Find out too late you have a big, stupid ketchup stain on your shirt. *Lash*. Miss the basket in PE. *Lash*. Try to say something funny and nobody laughs. *Lash*. Forget your homework. *Lash*. *Lash*. *Lash*."

Simon was quiet for a minute, then he said, "Five, six, seven, eight."

"What?" I said.

"Five, six, seven, eight," Simon repeated. "Fifty-six is seven times eight. That's how you can remember seven times eight. If you just think about five, six, seven, eight, it helps you remember. Get it? It's a trick. There are a lot of tricks if you want to learn multiplication tables.

"I could teach you," he went on excitedly. "I could show you the POWER OF DISCIPLINE." Trumpet flare. "You could be perfect. Well, within striking distance, anyway. By my calculations, sixty-five point six percent perfect."

"Only sixty-five percent?" I said.

"Well," Simon said, sounding a bit like his old self, "you are only human."

I stared up at the sky. A few clouds drifted by, thin and aimless. Five, six, seven, eight, I thought. That was a pretty good trick.

"I don't know, Simon. It sounds kind of hard being perfect."

"It's worth a try," he said.

I thought about my dad. About him saying I didn't even try. I wondered if he was right. Maybe I did give up too easily. Maybe if I just learned to be more like Simon, I could show him that I could be good at things, too. Maybe it was worth a try.

I took a deep breath.

"OK," I said. "Teach me the POWER OF DISCIPLINE."

B*RIIIINNGGG!!! BRIIIINNGGG!!!*

"Rise and shine," said Simon pleasantly, looking down at me from the upper bunk.

"Repeat after me," he said. "Every day in every way, I'm getting better and better."

Why had I ever agreed to learn the POWER OF DISCIPLINE? The second I did, Simon had turned cheerful, encouraging, and patient.

It was terrible.

"I keep my commitments," said Simon. "Repeat after me."

"I keep my commitments," I muttered.

He nodded. He continued to look at me. Bright-eyed. Helpful. He was not going to go away.

"Every day in every way, I'm getting better and better," I croaked.

He hopped from the bunk and began to do jumping jacks. I could see his feet moving crisply back and forth as I peered out from under the blanket.

I creaked to a sitting position.

Simon smiled encouragingly. I stood up and began to jump beside him.

Music trumpeted from his ears. Some kind of marching song.

We did jumping jacks and push-ups and ran in place; then we marched off to the bathroom to brush our teeth.

Then we came back to the bedroom, put everything away, and made the beds, the sheets and blankets pulled tight as a drum.

"Oh my," said Mom, appearing at the doorway. "Doesn't this look nice. Thank you, Simon."

"Chip did it, too," said Simon.

"Really?" Mom smiled politely, but she didn't really believe it. "Well, you boys have certainly earned your breakfast."

At breakfast, I just copied what Simon did. Napkin in lap. No grabbing of cereal bowl and draining the milk with a loud slurp. No fingers.

Dad, who was busy shoving eggs onto his fork with his fingers, paused and stared at me.

"Are you all right?" he asked.

"Every day in every way, I'm getting better and better," I said.

Dad ignored that.

"Chip, I know we had some words the other night. I admit I was angry about Simon, perhaps I spoke a bit harshly, but I really think it's time you got back to swim workout," he said.

"Dad, Simon's your winner. You don't need me."

Dad tried to think of something to say, but he couldn't.

The funny thing is I meant it. I'd never swim as good as Simon. My dad *didn't* need me, and when he and Simon left for swim practice, I gave them a big cheerful wave and went back in the house and stood staring at a crack in the wall.

"Every day in every way, I'm getting better and better," I said to myself.

"Better and better at being a loser," said a little voice inside me.

I began to do push-ups just to show the little voice that he was wrong. I got all the way up to five.

Then I got an idea. I grabbed my backpack, my swim trunks, and a towel and headed out the door.

On our walk up the hill to Bryant that afternoon, Simon drilled me on the multiplication tables.

Then I sat in class and waited. At last Ms. Broadbeam got to our multiplication drill. She pointed around the room and fired out the problems.

"Five times six?"

"Thirty," shouted Sally Johnston.

"Four times nine?"

"Forty-nine," shouted Brad Hornbill, like always.

"Seven times eight?" She swung her finger toward me.

"Fifty-six," I announced. "Seven times eight is fifty-six."

"Very good, Chip!" she warbled. "Very good. That's a hard one, isn't it, class?"

"It's not so hard," I said politely, "if you remember the trick."

And I told the class about the five, six, seven, eight thing.

"My, that is a good trick. Thank you, Chip." Ms. Broadbeam beamed.

The class looked kind of impressed.

Maybe this POWER OF DISCIPLINE thing wasn't so bad after all.

BRIIIINNGGG!!!

I jolted upright. *BRIIIINNGGG!!!*

"Rise and shine," said Simon.

"Every day in every way, I'm getting better and better," I groaned, crawling out of bed.

Every day started the same. Up and out of bed. Jumping jacks, push-ups, bed made. Hearty breakfast. Dad and Simon off to swim practice.

Every day Dad tried to make me come to swim practice.

Every day I shook my head no, and then after they left, I got my swim trunks and towel and headed out the door.

I went to Green Lake all by myself, and I swam back and forth, back and forth from the shore to the log. I didn't have any way to time myself, but I tried to push just a little bit harder each time, like Simon had said.

Afterward I fished. I got pretty good—I caught a fish or two every day, but I always threw them back. I just liked sitting there and plunking the line in and watching the water ripple away. You could think about things like how long exactly could you hear a plane passing overhead and could you figure out the exact second when you couldn't hear it anymore and how many kinds of green could you find and why was anything the way it was anyway.

I always left in time to beat Simon and Dad home. My hair dried out on the bike ride home, and I shoved my towel and suit into the dryer. I guess I just didn't want anyone to know I was swimming. Since I wasn't going to practice anymore, it was nobody's business, and maybe I was getting better, maybe I wasn't. It was just something I wanted to do.

Mrs. Cranston was finally back from a trip to a big

gardening show, so I usually went over to work with her in her yard. She'd come back with lots of ideas, and she liked asking me about them. She said my imagination was good for helping her figure out how the little things we planted would look when they were big a year or so from now.

In the meantime, Westerwood was winning every meet—mainly because of Simon. Dad and Coach Benjamin had started out cautiously—entering him in just that one relay event against Viewridge. But after that, they put him into every event they could. And he always came in first.

The other parents started to grumble. They didn't care if it wasn't in the rule book. Robots shouldn't be allowed to compete. Dad and the coach just shrugged. Simon kept on swimming, and Westerwood kept on winning.

Finally Westerwood had one last meet with Viewridge, and then it was on to the City Championships.

"I can see that All-City Trophy with your name on it, Simon," said Dad, waving toward the display case in the media room. "Right next to mine."

He slid his eyes over toward me.

"Won't that be nice," he said loudly. "Wouldn't it be nice to have a second big shining trophy up here."

"That will be swell, Dad," said Simon.

I just went on watching my show. That *would* be swell, but it had nothing to do with me.

For some reason, Dad sighed.

That evening, while Simon and I played Universal Mayhem on our hand modules and Mom read in the chaise longue, Dad tried to get the voice-activated backyard barbecue to behave.

"Medium rare," he ordered.

"Affirmative," said the barbecue, but then it sent up a huge flame. Dad snatched out the hamburger patties. They were charred cinders.

"I'll go make some more," said Simon, going inside.

"Rare!" Dad yelled at the barbecue.

The flame went out.

"You're going to the scrap heap!" cried Dad.

It made a rude noise at him.

Dad slumped and turned away. He usually didn't give up this easily.

"Are you OK, Dad?" I asked. "Is Simon's swimming going OK?"

"Fantastic," he said in a dull voice. "We're going to destroy Viewridge tomorrow," he said in the same uninterested voice.

"Gosh, Dad, that's great . . . isn't it?"

"It's not the same," he suddenly said. "Not the same as with you."

"I'm never going to win a trophy, Dad."

"That's OK," he said. "That's not the main thing."

"Oh, come on, Dad."

"No, really. There's something you should know. Something I need to tell you. Chip, I, ah, I never . . ."

Just then Simon popped out with a new platter of hamburger patties.

"Here you are, Father."

"Thank you, Simon," he said, looking a little relieved at the interruption.

Dad eyed the barbecue.

"Medium," he said. Nothing.

"Pretty please," he muttered.

A nice little flame flared up.

He flopped the burgers on the grill.

"Well, anyway," he said, "maybe you'd like to come to the meet tomorrow?"

He looked over at me. He looked a little bit like Simon did when he wanted to be friends.

"I'd really like it if you would," he said quietly.

"Well, OK," I said.

Mom glanced up from her book and smiled.

The next morning Dad and Simon left early so Simon could warm up. It was the last meet between Viewridge and Westerwood. We'd beaten Viewridge for the first time ever in our first matchup, and now Viewridge was out for blood. But nobody was very worried. Not with Simon on our side.

But when I got there, Dad and Coach Benjamin were huddled anxiously in a corner of the locker room. Simon sat before them, stiff and pale.

"That swine!" cried Dad.

"What's going on?" I asked.

"Butch Neeman got an ERIK3000," Dad said darkly.

"Latest model-boy robot," said Coach Benjamin. "Brand-new, just on the market. Supposedly better than the Simonson XX."

Leave it to the Neemans to get an even better robot!

"The ERIK3000 does have an advanced chip," said Simon, "but like all model-boy robots, some development over time is required."

"What's that mean?" Coach Benjamin asked.

"They have to learn. They have to be trained," said Simon.

Dad and Coach Benjamin looked at each other. They'd been working with Simon for weeks. The ERIK3000 had just come out.

"Are you sure?" asked the coach.

"Well, that is the whole point of the model-boy and model-girl robots. You are purchasing a perfect child, of course—but one who does need some guidance and instruction, so that parents can experience the gratification of successful parenting. A totally artificial experience, of course, but then desperate, incompetent parents will pay a tidy sum for—"

Simon suddenly stopped and glanced at Dad.

"Hmmph." Dad frowned, but Coach Benjamin looked relieved.

"Come on," he said. "Let's go see this ERIK3000."

When we got outside, a huge crowd was gathered around something at one end of the pool. Butch Neeman and Mike were at the center, but when Butch saw us, he smiled and pushed through the crowd toward us.

"Well, well," he said. "So glad you finally got here.

Got a new 'son' here I want you to meet. The latest addition to our family *and* to the Viewridge team." His smile was kind of like a shark's smile. "I'd like you to meet Erik."

We all turned our eyes to the boy, who stepped up beside Mr. Neeman.

He was as trim as a boxwood hedge, with a white-blond crewcut, cold blue eyes, and a chin like a block of steel. His lip curled up as if he smelled something bad.

"He's no eleven-year-old," cried Coach Benjamin. "Look at those muscles."

"He's officially eleven. It says so right here on his papers." Butch Neeman whipped out his ERIK3000 certificate of ownership and handed it over.

Meanwhile, the ERIK3000 and Simon studied each other.

Simon swelled his muscles to their fullest and added a nice golden tan to his skin. Erik sneered and inflated his own muscles. They were twice the size of Simon's! And his sudden tan was the exquisite golden brown of a perfectly roasted marshmallow. His waist got thinner, too.

"How do you like my new brother?" said Mike, patting Erik on the back.

Erik looked at Mike like he was maybe a bug. Mike kept smiling like he and Erik were best buddies, but I noticed he quickly took his hand down.

"See you at the races," Mr. Neeman said, walking away with a laugh.

I looked over at my dad. He looked kind of greenish. Suddenly I felt sort of sorry for him. Maybe he couldn't help it that he cared so much. Maybe beating Butch Neeman when they were kids had been like me catching that first fish—a feeling so good that you just wanted to feel it again. I wondered if I'd force my kid to catch fish when I was grown up. And if he didn't like it, maybe I'd be just as baffled as my dad was with me.

"Hey, Simon's the best," I said. "He's going to beat Erik, just like you clobbered Mr. Neeman when you were kids."

Dad stared at me for a moment. He tried to smile, but actually he looked even greener.

There was a whole afternoon of races that day, human races, but nobody paid any attention to them. We were all waiting for Simon and Erik to face each other for the first time in the eighth race of the day—the ten-to-eleven-year-old-boys breaststroke.

Finally the announcer called the start of Event 8. There were four other swimmers in the event, including Mike Neeman, but everyone knew they didn't have a chance.

Both Simon and Erik stepped up onto the starting blocks. Erik stumbled just a bit, and Simon glanced over at my dad. Erik hadn't been fully trained yet.

Even so, he clasped his hands together over his head like he was already celebrating his victory. The Viewridge fans whistled and stomped.

Simon glared at him, then raised his hands over his head. We all screamed and shouted.

"Kill him!" roared Dad. Then, when some parents glanced his way, he added like a good sport, "May the best machine win."

"Take your marks," said the starter.

Simon bent to grasp the starting block. Erik glanced at him, then quickly did the same.

"He's just copying Simon!" I said.

BANG!

Erik was a second behind Simon in his dive, and he hit at an angle that was a little too steep. Even Mike came out of his dive ahead of him. But then he and all the other humans were quickly left behind as Erik gained on Simon.

They reached the end of the pool and executed their flip turns. Simon was in the lead. No surprise there—after all, this was the breaststroke. Nobody could beat Simon in the breaststroke. But then, slowly, Erik began to gain ground.

With each stroke, he more perfectly copied Simon's stroke, Simon's rhythm. And he had just a little bit more muscle power to add.

We watched in horror as he caught up with, then

passed Simon, touching the edge of the pool a fraction of a second before Simon to win the race.

"What happened?" Dad cried, rushing up to Simon as he pulled himself dripping from the pool.

"He has the new Super-Accelerated Learning Curve program," said Simon. "All he has to do is see something once, and he's programmed."

And so it went for the rest of the meet. Erik just watched whatever Simon did, and Simon's weeks of working to perfect his strokes and strategy and timing were instantly absorbed.

"Copycat!" I cried once, but even I knew it was a pretty feeble insult.

Erik didn't care. He might be a copycat, but he also led Viewridge to victory over Westerwood in race after race. As he strode from the swimming pool at the end of the meet, he looked at me for the first time ever.

"First I copy," he said quietly so no one else could hear, "then I crush."

Then he strode away with the rest of the Viewridge team straggling behind him.

Chapter 13

"There's got to be a way to beat that monster," Dad raged at dinner that night.

Simon looked bad. His hair was actually kind of messy, and I noticed a splotch of gravy on his shirt.

"The Super-Accelerated Learning Curve, or SALC, device was in development when I left the factory," said Simon. "I don't see how Robots Inc. got it on the market so fast."

"Cyborg Corp. said *you* were the most advanced," Dad grumbled.

"Extraordinary products for ordinary people," Simon chimed without much conviction.

"Well," said Mother, trying to stay cheerful, "I always say, 'If at first you don't succeed, try, try again.' There's always the All-City Championships!"

Nobody said anything.

Later, while Simon and I were doing the dishes—our sonic dishwasher had quit working a week ago—we heard Dad on the phone in the hall.

It sounded like he was talking to Cyborg Corp.

"Well, when *will* you have the new chips available?"

Mumble, buzz, said the voice on the other end of the line, and Dad said loudly, "Oh, yeah? Well, I could have bought a new car for the same amount of money!"

Mumble, buzz.

"A really good car!" cried Dad, and he slammed down the phone.

That night as we got ready for bed, Simon was awful quiet. He fiddled through a couple of radio channels in his head, then sighed and clicked his receiver off.

"You can't be perfect at everything," I said.

"You don't understand," he cried. "I'm obsolete! I'm an outdated model. Now everyone will want an ERIK3000."

"Not necessarily," I said. "I think you're way more likable."

"You do?" Simon lifted his head hopefully.

"Sure. I mean, winning isn't everything."

Simon slumped back down.

"When you buy a model son, and they don't come cheap, well, the customer expects to win," he muttered.

"No, that's not true," I said. "Mom and Dad like you for yourself, not just because you're a winner."

Simon didn't stir, and I couldn't blame him—even I didn't believe it. Dad hadn't paid half a year's salary to come in second.

"Besides," I said, trying another approach, "who says you're going to lose? You still have a week before the City Championships."

Simon shrugged.

"Every day in every way," I reminded him, "you *can* get just a little bit better. That's the POWER OF DISCIPLINE."

I made a trumpet call through my rolled-up hand.

Simon raised his head. He looked at me, and suddenly his eyes blazed. He took his ear and started to twist it.

"What are you doing!?"

"I'm setting the alarm early," he declared. "Tomorrow I'm getting up at five o'clock. I don't have a second to waste."

By the time I got up at seven, Simon and my dad were long gone.

So, as usual, I went alone to Green Lake. No way was Simon getting a day off now, and Towler wouldn't be back from camp until the weekend.

I did my laps, pushing just a little harder with each stroke back and forth till I was out of breath. I was pretty sure I was getting faster. It wasn't so hard if you did it bit by bit. Sort of like eating a giant hot dog. I mean, it's not like you could just cram the whole thing in your mouth, but if you took tiny, steady bites, you could eat a lot that way.

Later, I went home for lunch, but still no Simon. So I went to school on my own. I kind of missed having him to walk with. It wasn't just because he helped drill me on things. I don't know, I just missed him—like he was a real person or something. Weird.

To my surprise, all the kids were talking about the swim championships. Usually nobody but the swimmers and their parents much cared.

"Didn't you see it on the news this morning?" asked Brenda. She pointed to a headline on the screen of the class computer.

"MAN VERSUS MACHINE. MACHINE WINS."

The story was about how Simon and now the ERIK3000 had taken over the summer swim league and how all the parents and swimmers were mad.

"No human has a chance," protested one parent in the story. "They're going to take over the world if we don't watch out."

But a scientist from the local university said, "What's all the fuss? Survival of the fittest, after all. As superior beings, they'll probably be kind to us. They'll probably keep some of us around as pets."

"No Cyborg product has ever harmed a human

being," said a computerized spokes-entity from the company. "We can't speak for Robots Inc. All I can say is our chips are bigger than their chips. BONG!"

The story predicted a big turnout at the All-City Championships. "Some are coming to protest," the story went on. "Some out of curiosity. Perhaps even a few to cheer on this new kind. No matter what, humankind can never feel the same."

Even Mrs. Cranston had heard about it.

As we planted a bed of purple coneflowers, she chatted.

"People are a bit crazy when it comes to sports," she said. "I'm sure I don't know why. Give me a person with a good green thumb any day."

She leaned back and surveyed the bed we'd planted. It looked pretty good, except for one bare patch.

"What about that spot?" I asked.

"Oh, I'll fill that in later when I see how all this works. Some things will come out; some things will get moved. You have to leave room for mistakes, you know."

I nodded, but I wasn't paying much attention.

"That's why we don't have to worry, you know," she said.

"Huh?"

"About robots. They can't make mistakes." She clicked her tongue.

"But that's a good thing, isn't it?"

"Oh my, no," she said. "They're stuck with only what can be imagined. We get to do the unimaginable. It's a lot more flexible, you know."

"Mrs. Cranston," I said, "you're weird."

"Thank you," she said happily, and began to put away the gardening tools.

"Still, it is too bad that you won't be in the race."

I shrugged. "Dad's got Simon for the race. Simon wins everything. That's all Dad really cares about."

Mrs. Cranston clicked her tongue some more. "He's never gotten over it, has he?"

"Gotten over what?"

"You know, the final race between him and Butch Neeman at the All-City—"

"Oh, yeah," I interrupted. "He has the trophy in our family room. I've heard a million times about how he beat the trunks off Butch Neeman."

Mrs. Cranston looked startled. "Is that what he told you?" she said.

"He loves to tell that story," I said.

She opened her mouth, then shut it. Finally she said, "Like I said, people get a bit crazy when it comes to sports."

"Fight! The robots are fighting!"

It was the big day. The All-City Swim Championships of Eastville. The pool was jam-packed. Parents, reporters, media crews, even the mayor, were crowded into the stands and around the pool deck.

But most of the swimmers and other kids were out back on the lawn behind the clubhouse, where Simon and Erik circled each other like fighting fish.

They had met up when Simon and I and Towler, who was back from camp, were walking to the boys' locker room from the parking lot. Mike and Erik had come down the other side of the lawn on their way to the locker room, too.

Simon and Erik had slowed and stared at each other. Eyes snapped. Chins squared.

Erik raised a finger and pointed it like an arrow at Simon.

"I challenge you," he said.

"Challenge accepted," said Simon.

"Come on, everybody!" A girl shouted into the locker rooms. "They're going to fight!"

Everyone came running.

We waited, breaths held, for them to pounce. I remembered how my punching Simon in the stomach hadn't made a dent.

The Battle of the Robots. This would be awesome! I looked over at Simon. His titanium jaw seemed to tremble, and I realized with a sudden worried feeling that fighting the Erik3000 wasn't exactly the same as fighting me.

"Pi to the fifth decimal?" Erik suddenly snapped.

"Three point one four one five nine," Simon snapped back. "Ten to the sixth power?"

"One million," sneered Erik, as if everyone knew that.

"Uh!" said a girl. "They're doing math problems!"

"You call this a fight?!" Brad Hornbill protested.

"Robots don't resort to physical violence," said Erik. "How primitive. That's what humans do."

He said *human* as though it was a dirty word.

"The capital of Kentucky," Simon cried, trying to catch him off guard.

"Frankfort." Erik didn't hesitate for a second.

Everyone groaned. This wasn't what we had in mind at all.

The questions and answers flew back and forth at

dizzying speed—some so complicated we had no idea what the question was, much less the answer. But some were simple, because you never knew exactly what a robot's programming and learning were. Maybe something simple had been missed.

But no matter what the question, neither hesitated for a moment. Neither could stump the other.

But then it looked like Simon's weeks of human training might pay off.

"Decibels from Hell," he suddenly cried.

He was remembering the Galactic Battle of the Bands.

Erik paused, frowned. His eyes began to scan back and forth. He was checking his data banks. Back and forth, back and forth went his eyes. Faster and faster. He'd never heard of them!

A couple of kids snickered. Everyone knew who the Decibels from Hell were.

"Do you concede?" Simon asked calmly.

Erik stopped scanning, but then to my surprise, he looked over at me. His eyes narrowed, and he stepped in front of me.

"Stand back," Simon ordered. "Remember the first law!"

Erik clenched his fingers into a fist and swung at my jaw. Faster than lightning, Simon's arm lashed out to stop his.

But Erik didn't throw a punch.

"Gotcha," he said, pulling up his arm and brushing his hair back, as if that's all he had planned to do in the first place.

I looked at Simon, who had gone white as paper. And then I noticed that his arm was still stuck out in front of him. It was frozen there.

"Servo-mechanical safety switch," said Erik to the crowd with a superior sneer. "Built into all robots. It detects intent to harm and locks up the offending member of the robot unit. Standard safety measure. Since I had no actual intent to harm, my switch did not kick in. The Simonson XX, however, intended to disable me for no permissible reason."

Then he swaggered on down to the locker room.

"Simon?" I said. "What happened?"

"He tricked me into a violent action. My arm is now locked in place. It can't be reactivated without a repair visit to the factory."

"You mean your arm is stuck there?"

Simon nodded miserably.

"What's going on?"

Several grown-ups, including my dad and Coach Benjamin, hurried up.

Dad saw Simon's arm and gasped.

"He's broken," I explained.

"Are you sure you can't move it?" Dad pushed on it, but it was as hard as a rod of steel.

He groaned, "That means . . ."

"I can't swim," Simon finished for him. "Someone else from the team will have to race in my place."

Everyone looked grim, and Coach Benjamin said, "Nobody can. There's nobody left on the team. There's nobody left on any of the teams."

"We all quit," said a boy.

"In protest," said a girl.

"The only, er, *entities* left in the race are Simon and Erik. Even all the Viewridge swimmers dropped out, because, well, Erik can do it all," she explained.

"We'll have to forfeit." Dad raised his fists toward the heavens. "We have no choice. We have no swimmers. No one's left on the roster!"

Everyone was real quiet for a moment, and that's when I said, "I am."

Everyone looked at me.

"I'm still on the roster," I said. "I didn't quit because I didn't know."

"Is he still on the team?" asked Dad.

"Well, officially, yes," said Coach Benjamin.

"Then Chip can race Erik," Towler said.

My dad and Coach Benjamin and everyone turned to look at me.

"But I don't have a chance," I said.

No one disagreed.

"I guess we'll just have to forfeit," said Coach Benjamin. Everyone sighed and turned away.

"I could try, though," I said.

They all turned back.

"Sure, I don't have a chance," I said. I suddenly felt something like a trumpet flaring inside me. "But I've lost more races than anyone here. And I can do it again!"

The crowd went wild. Cheering and screaming, they marched with me down to the boys' locker room.

A drop of water fell from the showerhead in the locker room and hit the bathroom tile with a lonely kind of *plunk*. After a moment, another one fell and then another.

I could hear each drop really well because I was in the locker room all by myself. Waiting. For the Big Race. And it was very quiet in there.

I'd told everybody I needed some time alone to get ready. They'd all trampled out of the room and were now waiting by the pool for me to come out.

"Man against machine," I heard a reporter saying into a mike just outside the locker room door. "Unfortunately, the only human competitor left has lost every race he's ever been in."

Hey, I hadn't lost every race; I just hadn't won any. But I supposed it was accurate enough for the media. I swallowed and wondered just how badly I would lose. How stupid would I look in front of all those people and reporters and media cameras? How stupid would I look in front of the world?

I tried to breathe. I was pretty sure I was going to throw up.

"Chip?"

I looked up. It was Dad.

"I know we should have forfeited," I said quickly. "I don't know what came over me. I, I—"

"I'm proud of you, Chip," Dad said.

"Really?" It kind of sounded like he meant it.

He sighed and sat down next to me on the bench.

"Chip, there's something I should have told you a long time ago."

There was a quiet moment when we could both hear the *plunk* of the shower. Dad ran his hand over his face.

"I never won the All-City Ten-to-Eleven-Year-Old-Boys Swim Championship of Eastville," he said.

"What?!"

"Butch Neeman clobbered me. Beat me by a good half a length. Maybe more."

"But your trophy!"

"It's a fake. I bought it at a garage sale and then had a fake little plate made."

"A fake?" I couldn't believe it. All those years of telling me how he beat Butch Neeman! "But why'd you do that?"

Dad put his face in his hands.

"I don't know," he muttered. "All my life, everything I have, everything I do, it's just secondhand, you know. Second-best. I've never even been promoted to supervisor."

I thought of all our stuff. The media center, our car, the snotty barbecue, even Simon, if you thought about it—all second-best.

"Like me," I said, it suddenly hitting me.

"No, not like you!" said Dad. "No, Chip, you're the best."

"But I'm not, Dad. I'm not the best at anything."

"You're the best thing I ever did," Dad said.

"But I never win, Dad."

"Yeah, and I wanted you to. I wanted you to be a winner, because, well, I wasn't."

"Were you supposed to beat Butch Neeman?" I asked. I wondered if he'd made it up about being a good swimmer, too.

Dad nodded. "Yeah, actually I was. I really was pretty good back then."

"What happened?"

Dad shook his head as if he couldn't believe it himself. "I started thinking about what it would be like to have five eyes."

"What?"

"I have this daydreaming thing," he said. "I wonder about things a lot. That's why I like being a mailman. You walk around and you can think, you know."

"That's what I do, too!" I said. "Daydream."

"I know," said Dad. "You got it from me, I'm afraid. I'm sorry. Daydreaming kind of gets in the way of, you know, being a winner at things."

Dad sighed.

"I like it," I said. "I like thinking weird things. I mean, what *would* it be like to have five eyes?"

"Very confusing," answered Dad solemnly, because he'd actually thought about it.

Then he looked at me. I couldn't help it. I started to grin. And then, suddenly, we were both laughing. Quietly at first, and then louder and louder until the sound of it bounced off the tiles, and we couldn't laugh anymore, and Dad ruffled my hair like he hadn't done in a long time. And then we were quiet for a while.

"I'm going to lose really bad, Dad," I finally said. "I mean, you know, an ERIK3000."

"Ah, who cares," he said. "You'll do the best you can, and that's good enough."

And this time I could tell he really did mean it.

I walked out into the sunlight. Hundreds of human faces and a dozen media cameras swiveled in my direction.

The crowd fell quiet, parting to let me through. It seemed like the whole town was there. To my surprise, Mrs. Cranston stood high in the stands, waving. Towler slapped me on the back as I went through. Mom pushed up her glasses and gave me a big, encouraging smile. And there near the pool was Simon with his arm thrust awkwardly before him.

"Good luck," he said.

"Thanks," I said. "Listen, I'm sorry about your arm. I mean, you were trying to protect me, and now after all your hard work, you don't get to race Erik."

"That's all right," he said. "It's not your fault. Besides, who knows—maybe you'll beat him."

We turned to look at Erik, who waited for me near the starting block.

"Maybe," I said, but we both knew it was impossible.

He was taller and stronger and smarter and infinitely superior to me in every way. He surveyed the crowd. His nostrils kind of quivered, and then he raised his arms straight up like in victory. After a moment, Mr. Neeman began to clap and then Mike, but it was quickly over because no one else clapped. Not even the rest of his own team.

And that's when I got my idea. It was a great idea,

really. A brilliant idea. An idea in a million, but I had no idea if it would work.

I walked over to Erik. Everyone was pretty surprised, but I stuck out my hand. Erik looked startled.

"You shake it," I explained to him. "To be a good sport."

He hesitated, then stuck out his hand, and while we were shaking I said something to him. Low, so nobody else could hear. He kind of blinked, then shrugged and gave my hand a hard squeeze. His eyes were cold marbles, and his smile was still superior. I guess he didn't care about what I said.

Oh, well. It had been worth a try.

"Swimmers ready."

We climbed onto the starting blocks.

"Take your marks."

We bent.

BANG!

We were off.

I got a good start with a clean, shallow dive, and I came up with a good, hard overhead stroke. Erik and I were actually even!

I dug in, pushing with each stroke as hard as I could. My flip turn was perfect, the best I'd ever done, but as I came out of it, I saw that Erik was well ahead. I swam the hardest I'd ever swum in my life. Harder than any race I'd been in. Harder than any time at Green Lake. My heart pounded like it would burst. There was no way I could win, but for once, I would give it my all.

Still it didn't matter. Erik was far ahead. He was one stroke from the finish. I closed my eyes and, with a last desperate burst of effort, I shot forward and slapped my palm against the pool edge.

I jerked my head out of the water, gasping for air. I thought I was going to die. I looked up expecting to see Erik scrambling from the water. All I saw were hundreds of human faces peering down at me. Their mouths were open. They were shouting something. It was my name.

"CHIP! CHIP! CHIP!"

Hands reached down and pulled me from the water.

I glanced back and, to my astonishment, Erik was still in the water.

He was in midstroke, his head turned to take a breath. His hand was a micron from the pool edge, but not quite touching it. He was breathing and blinking, but his body was totally frozen. He was unable to move another inch. He looked puzzled.

I didn't have a chance to notice anything more because two big men grabbed me and hoisted me to their shoulders and carried me around the pool! Everyone shouted and laughed and slapped each other on the back.

"Man against machine," crowed a reporter into her mike. "Man wins!"

For the first time in my life, I was a winner! My idea had worked.

"Hooray for Chip! Hip hip hooray!!" everyone shouted.

I was more than a winner. I was a hero!

Swarms of people came up to shake my hand. A bunch of reporters asked me questions. It was cool. Mom smiled at me like she never doubted I would win. Towler pushed through the crowd, grinning from ear to ear.

"Way to go!" he said. "You were awesome. You practically beat him even if he hadn't broken down."

We both looked over at Erik. He was still there, still floating just a hair from winning the race. But it was too late. He would never win the race, not in this universe.

"Come on. Let's get this danged thing home," groused Mr. Neeman.

He and Mike towed the quiet, uncomplaining Erik to the pool steps, and Mr. Neeman jumped in and hoisted him out.

"Lightweight alloy! Bull-oney!" he grunted, struggling to lift the robot from the water.

Then he and Mike each grabbed a different end of Erik and, staggering with the weight of him, carried him stiff as a board from the pool. Erik just blinked and looked lost. People in the crowd hooted and clapped.

Simon stood by, watching. The way his arm was frozen, it almost looked like he was saluting Erik, and I wondered how he felt about a fellow robot losing to a human. But when he turned and saw me, he grinned and shot up his thumb.

I talked to some more reporters and shook about a million more hands, and finally the crowd started to thin out, and my mom and dad came up.

"Congratulations," said Dad.

"Funny how that Erik broke down at the last minute," said Coach Benjamin. "Just goes to show you can't count on machines. No offense," he added quickly to Simon, who stood nearby.

"He's not broken," I said. "He's lost in a logic loop."

"Huh?"

"Yeah, remember how I shook his hand before the race?"

"Very sporting of you," said Coach Benjamin.

"Well, I also said something to him. I didn't think it had worked, but then it did."

"What did you say to him?" asked Mom.

"Something simple, but something impossible for a robot to deal with. I simply told him that if you're perfect, no one likes you, so you're not really perfect, because if you were perfect, everyone would like you. So to be truly perfect, you have to be imperfect."

I looked around at everyone and smiled.

"He didn't know whether to win the race or to lose. It blew his logic circuits. Only people are crazy enough to handle something like that!"

Simon blinked, and I suddenly worried that maybe I'd put him into a logic loop, too, but then his eyes glinted.

"Yes, of course, it's perfectly logical. Since I'm not perfect, I am more perfect than the ERIK3000!"

And he leapt in the air, messing his hair up and everything.

A week later, they held the awards banquet for the swim league. They had decided to eliminate all robot scores from the final awards, but even so, our team got quite a few trophies for its performance during the season. And Simon got a special award for "Hardest Worker."

Then I got called up, and while everyone clapped and hollered, they handed me the giant silver trophy for winning the All-City Ten-to-Eleven-Year-Old-Boys Swim Championship of Eastville.

My dad looked like he was going to blow up like a balloon and burst with pride. And he shook Butch

Neeman's hand so hard afterward that Mr. Neeman's eyes bulged.

Mom smiled and patted me on the back when I got back to the table, but I had made her a lot prouder the day before when I brought home my grades from summer school.

"There are B's here," she had said, pulling her glasses off and cleaning them and then putting them back on to look again. Then she'd given me a big hug, which I let her do even though I'm now officially a sixth grader.

I couldn't believe it. I'd passed summer school; Mrs. Cranston's garden was in full, glorious bloom; and I had won the All-City Ten-to-Eleven-Year-Old-Boys Swim Championship of Eastville in *this* universe! It had turned out to be a pretty good summer after all.

When we got home, Dad started to take his giant silver trophy down to put mine up.

"Why are you taking that away?" I asked.

"I can't believe I was so childish," Dad said. "I'm sorry. How embarrassing to live such a lie."

"I don't think it's a lie," I said.

"Chip, I freely admit it now. I did not win the All-City Ten-to-Eleven-Year-Old-Boys Swim Championship of Eastville. I lost. I can accept that now. I'm moving on."

"Dad, take a look at your trophy."

"Huh?"

Dad peered at the little silver nameplate. It read: TO THE BEST DAD IN THE WORLD.

He looked at me. Mom and I had changed the plate one day when Dad was at work.

"Why, I—I—" Dad cleared his throat. Blinked. Tried to act like he had a cough or something. Finally, he got a tissue and blew his nose with a big honk.

"I've never been the best at anything before," he said. "Thanks, Chip."

"Sure, Dad," I said.

He put his big silver trophy up next to mine.

Dad thought we should send Simon back to the factory for a refund.

We all sat on the brown fake-leather couch in the family room, watching a show about groundhogs on the media center.

Simon's arm was still stuck out before him, but that made it convenient for him to hold the remote control.

"After all, he's broken," said Dad.

"I'm afraid I'm not quite the product you were promised," Simon agreed sadly.

"You can't send him back," I protested. "He's my brother. He belongs with us."

Dad hesitated. "What do *you* want, Simon?"

"I would be honored to remain a member of this family. *'An extraordinary family of ordinary people. DONG!'*" said Simon.

"We'll just get a repair, then. For the arm," said Dad. I could see his eyes beginning to glint. "And perhaps an upgrade."

"Dad," I said, "we like Simon just the way he is."

Mom nodded and laid a couple of napkins over Simon's arm for us to use with our snacks.

"Oh, all right. Just the arm then. We'll get the arm fixed, but otherwise I'll tell them we want Simon back, factory defects and all."

Mom, Simon, and I settled back happily.

Dad banged on the remote to change the channel.

"Oh, look," said Mom.

There was a commercial on the screen.

Get a PAUL! The Perfect Dad!
He plays catch with you!
He tells tales . . . with a moral!
He never has gas!
Yes, it's Paul the Robot. You'll grow up normal, after all.
Order yours today!

"It's a Perfect Dad Robot," I said.

"Yes, well." Dad quickly clicked off the media

center. "You know, we shouldn't be in here on such a beautiful day. How about you, me, and Simon going fishing? You can show me that special fishing hole of yours."

Simon nodded eagerly and jumped up.

"Did I ever tell you boys about the time I caught a brown spotted stickleback?" Dad asked as we gathered up our gear. "It was so big—"

"Is this going to be a tall tale, Dad?" I said.

"Well . . ." Dad looked a bit uncomfortable, but then he brightened. "But it doesn't have a moral!"

"Swell," I said.

"Let's go, boys," he said.

And he put his arms around our shoulders—father and sons—just like they do on TV.